In Darkest Night

JUSTICE LEAGUE™

In Darkest Night

by

MICHAEL JAN FRIEDMAN

Based on a story idea
by Rich Fogel

BANTAM BOOKS
NEW YORK • TORONTO • LONDON • SYDNEY • AUCKLAND

IN DARKEST NIGHT

A Bantam Book/August 2002

ISBN: 0-553-48771-X

Published simultaneously in the United States and Canada

Bantam Books is an imprint of Random House Children's Books, a division of Random House, Inc. BANTAM BOOKS and the rooster colophon are registered trademarks of Random House, Inc. Bantam Books, 1540 Broadway, New York, New York 10036.

PRINTED IN THE UNITED STATES OF AMERICA

OPM 10 9 8 7 6 5 4 3 2 1

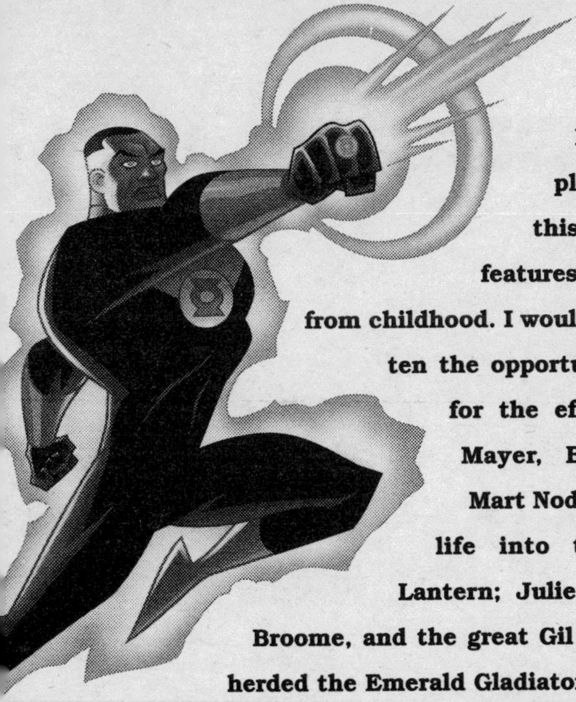

It was my great pleasure to write this book because it features my favorite hero from childhood. I would never have gotten the opportunity were it not for the efforts of Sheldon Mayer, Bill Finger, and Mart Nodell, who breathed life into the first Green Lantern; Julie Schwartz, John Broome, and the great Gil Kane, who shepherded the Emerald Gladiator into the sixties; Alfred Bester, who came up with Green Lantern's oath; the most excellent Denny O'Neil, who gave Green Lantern breadth and depth in the seventies; Neal Adams, who was the first to draw John Stewart; Dave Van Domelen and Inge Heyer, my science gurus; Justice League Producer Rich Fogel, who contributed this book's gem of an outline; Bruce Timm and his team at Warner Bros. Animation, whose graphics make my son's jaw drop; and the inestimable Charlie Kochman, who looked remarkably like Abin Sur as he sat in his spaceship and entrusted me with this assignment.

PROLOGUE

Dave Van Domelen had always loved the stars.

His childhood buddies had wanted to become firemen and baseball players, deep-sea divers and race car drivers. But Van Domelen had never been interested in any of those professions. For as long as he could remember, he had wanted to be an astronomer.

And he did whatever he had to in order to become one. He studied astronomy in high school, college, and graduate school. He spent his summers visiting observatory after observatory. He taught. He helped conduct research.

Finally, Van Domelen got a job at the kind of place he had always dreamed about. He was named assistant director of the prestigious Kane-Broome Institute for Space Studies in Coast City, California.

Kane-Broome studied the galaxy with the help of an immense telescope that had been placed in orbit around the Earth. The telescope, known as Solarac, was able to do more than pick up light from other stars. Because it was located outside Earth's atmosphere, Solarac was also able to detect gamma radiation and tiny particles that were constantly being ejected from Earth's sun.

The information gathered by Solarac was fed back to the Kane-Broome Institute, where it was stored and analyzed by a powerful computer. There Van Domelen and his fellow scientists had a chance to go over it, learning more about our sun, our solar system, and the rest of the universe in the process.

But Van Domelen wasn't content just to pore over computer data. Every night he took a turn at the bank of television monitors hooked up to the institute's computer, watching and hoping that something interesting would happen while he was there.

He did that for more than six months. But in all that time, nothing of interest took place. Nothing of even *mild* interest.

All Van Domelen ever saw on the monitors was normal solar activity. Unusual events like flares—sudden leaps and spurts of fiery solar gases—always seemed to take place when somebody else was manning the monitors.

And yet there he was again on a cool night in mid-October, sitting in front of the same gray mainframe computer and the same silent monitors, drinking the same black coffee out of the same kind of Styrofoam cup. But after more than six months of watching and hoping, Van Domelen was beginning to wonder if he was wasting his time.

When am I finally going to see something? he asked himself. He leaned closer to the biggest of the screens, the one that displayed a picture of the entire sun. *When am I going to witness something special?*

The scientist had barely completed the thought when he got his wish. Right before his eyes, the sun's surface seemed to erupt with a flare that was bigger, brighter, and more powerful than anything he could ever have imagined. It climbed so far into space, it looked like a long, slender finger on a giant, golden hand.

And the flare didn't subside right away, either. It kept erupting for what must have been a full minute.

Then, finally, it began to diminish in size and intensity. Eventually, it became just another part of the sun's aura again.

Feeling a thrill of excitement, the scientist checked some of the smaller monitors to find out the flare's measurements. As it turned out, it was every bit as impressive as it had looked. Kane-Broome had been in operation for six and a half years and nothing ever recorded there had even come close to this.

How lucky can I get? Van Domelen asked himself.

All his patience had been worth it. He couldn't wait to tell Dr. Giella, the director of the institute. He was sure his boss would be excited beyond words.

But as he reached for the telephone, Van Domelen's elbow hit his coffee cup and knocked it over. Hot, dark brown liquid spread across the table in front of him, threatening to damage its collection of keyboards and point-and-click mice.

"Whoa!" he cried, frantically snatching up the equipment before it could get wet.

He put it all on a shelf next to the table. Then he went to get some paper towels from the supply room down the hall. It took a few minutes for him to reach the supply room, a few more to find the paper towels, and a few more still to return to the control center.

By then, the unexpected had turned into the unbelievable.

The computer's gray exterior was crackling with a web of blue energy that looked as if it were trying to eat the mainframe alive. The same thing was happening to the bank of monitors. Black plumes of smoke were rising here and there, and the room was filled with the acrid scent of superheated metal.

"No!" Van Domelen roared, dropping his roll of paper towels.

What had happened while he was gone? Surely a spilled cup of coffee hadn't caused all *this*?

Searching for a clue, his eyes were drawn to the monitor screens—the big one in particular. It wasn't showing him a picture of the sun anymore. It was scrolling a series of bright red codes that looked like the commands found in a computer program.

Van Domelen understood enough of it to know what the commands meant. It was a repair sequence.

Solarac had been designed with the ability to take any part that might have gotten damaged and reconstruct it so it would work again. That was what it was doing now.

But what could have caused so much damage? Solarac had been working fine until a few moments ago.

Van Domelen studied the information on another monitor until he got an answer to his question. Apparently, the telescope had been hit with a burst of radiation—and not the kind that normally came out of the sun. This was a kind of radiation the computer couldn't seem to identify.

The *flare*, the scientist thought. Was it possible that it had been more than just big and impressive-looking? Had it released a wave of mysterious energy powerful enough to damage Solarac?

Van Domelen squinted as he watched the electric-blue web sizzle across the face of the computer. Whatever had hit the telescope, it hadn't stopped there. It had detected Solarac's data stream and sent an energy charge all the way back to Kane-Broome.

The scientist had never heard of anything like that before. But then, he had never seen a solar flare of such huge proportions either.

By then, Solarac had gone a long way toward rebuilding itself. But if the codes Van Domelen was reading were correct, it wasn't just rebuilding a *little*. It was rebuilding *everything*.

Solarac wasn't even a telescope anymore, he realized. A chill went up his spine. It was becoming some other kind of device entirely.

Then the scientist realized something else. Solarac's position in space was changing. It wasn't staying in orbit the way it was supposed to. It was coming back to Earth—and at a frightening speed.

A machine as powerful and complex as Solarac with a new body and a new mission? Van Domelen couldn't imagine what it would look like when it got there. He couldn't even begin to guess what kind of behavior it might exhibit.

But he found himself shivering at the thought of it.

CHAPTER 1

John Stewart knew he was having trouble with his memory again when he saw the collection of pale, orange fruit sitting in its crude wooden box.

He stopped in front of the fruit stand and stared at the fruit for a while. Then, as cars and trucks and people streamed past him, each making a particular kind of noise, he took a piece out of the box.

He held it up to the sunlight. He turned it over in his hand. He even tried smelling it, which wasn't an easy task with all the other interesting smells in his old neighborhood competing for his attention.

But even after John had done all that, he shook his head. He was sure he had once known the name of this fruit. But for the life of him, he couldn't remember what it was.

It didn't alarm him that his memory had some gaps in it. After all, he had patrolled space for years as a Green Lantern, fighting threats to the peaceful inhabitants of world after far-flung world. Only recently had he decided to return to Earth, the place of his birth.

In the time John had spent among the stars, he had become familiar with a hundred or more different species. He could say "Get back, I'll protect you!" in the languages of six dozen planets. He had filed away at least a thousand alien names, some of which he could barely wrap his mouth around.

But he had forgotten a few of the words he had used on Earth—simple words that he used to say without even thinking. And one of them was the name of a pale, orange fruit with a sweet smell and a soft, yielding kind of flesh.

"Something wrong?" asked the plump little woman who ran the fruit stand.

The Green Lantern shook his head. "Nothing."

He had always been the independent type. He felt uncomfortable asking for help from others.

"Yes, there is," the woman told him.

He looked at her. "There is?"

"Yes indeed." She took his left hand in both of hers. "There's no wedding ring on this finger. I'd say there's something wrong when a big, handsome man like yourself doesn't have a wife."

John frowned. "I've . . . been away on business a lot. Haven't had much time for a social life."

It was true. Green Lanterns dedicated themselves to their work. There was no room for anything else in their lives. It was a lonely existence at times, but someone had to do it.

"Well, then," said the woman, "you should *make* time. If I were you, I'd—"

John didn't hear the rest of her advice because an alarm had gone off in his ear—an alarm none of the neighborhood people around him could hear.

"John," said a deep, haunting voice, "this is—"

"I know who it is," John interrupted.

His name was J'onn J'onzz, and he was calling from a place in orbit around the Earth—a Watchtower set up by the Justice League. John and J'onn were both charter members of the group. J'onn lived in the Watchtower because he was the last surviving member of his Martian species.

To some people, J'onn might have seemed strange and maybe even frightening, with his green skin and his deep-set red eyes. But not to a Green Lantern. John had seen a lot stranger and a lot more frightening aliens in his travels.

"What's wrong?" he asked the Martian Manhunter.

"You've heard of Solarac?"

"Of course," John replied. He and his fellow Justice Leaguers could see it sometimes from their Watchtower, its lenses glinting in the unfiltered sunlight.

"Of course *what*?" asked the fruit stand lady.

John ignored her. "What about it?" he asked J'onn.

"Something has happened to it. The device has somehow reconfigured itself and is attacking Coast City."

Attacking Coast City? A *telescope?* John thought he had heard it all, but that was a new one on him.

"How could that happen?" he asked.

"From what I can gather, Solarac is absorbing energy. Coast City has that in great abundance."

It was as good an explanation as any.

"Superman is out in space," the Martian continued, "but I'm alerting the rest of the League."

"I'm on it," John said. "See you in Coast City."

By then, the fruit stand lady was staring at him good and hard. "Coast City?" she echoed. "Why would you want to see me *there*?"

John didn't have time to explain. He just willed

his ring—the one on the middle finger of his right hand—to turn his street clothes back into his Green Lantern uniform.

But before he left the stand, he had to ask a question. "That fruit," he said, pointing to the one that had baffled him, "what's it called?"

The fruit stand lady was staring at him with eyes as wide as Frisbees. No doubt she had never seen a super hero up close before. "A mango," she muttered. "It's called a mango."

"Mango," John repeated. He made a sound of disgust. How could he have forgotten something so simple?

With a burst of willpower, he rose into the air and rocketed off in the direction of Coast City.

John was more than a mile out of town when he remembered—he hadn't charged his ring in some time. The ring was the source of his power. Under his guidance, it could project beams and barriers of seething green energy. The last thing he wanted to do was run out of that energy during a brawl with a powerful enemy.

He looped back to the neighborhood, shot through a narrow space between two buildings, and entered the window he had left open in his apartment. It was a simple place, not much furniture or anything. But then, he had gotten used to traveling light during his days of patrolling space with the Green Lantern Corps.

Besides, there was really only one piece of furniture that mattered to John—and at the moment, it was invisible. Moving his hand over what appeared to be an empty table, he found it with his fingertips.

The thing was smooth like metal and cold to the touch, with both flat and rounded surfaces. When he pressed his ring against it, the contact made it appear before his eyes.

It was a lantern, glowing with an emerald light that bathed the entire room in its splendor. A *green* lantern.

John knew he didn't have to say anything while he was charging his ring. Just pressing it against the lantern would do the trick. But he always said something anyway.

"In brightest day, in darkest night, no evil shall escape my sight. Let those who worship evil's might, beware my power . . . Green Lantern's light."

It was the motto of the Green Lantern Corps, a reminder to every being who had been given a ring by the mysterious Guardians of the Universe that it was his or her duty to stand up to evil in all its forms. And not just sometimes . . . *all* the time.

That was the most difficult part of being a Green Lantern—the need to be on guard twenty-four hours a day, seven days a week. He could never just relax the way other people did. He always had to be ready to fly off at a moment's notice.

Sometimes John wondered what it would be like to have a family like other guys his age. He would picture himself barbecuing in the backyard, watching his kids play ball while his wife hugged him and told him what a terrific cook he was.

Then he would get wind of someone in need of help and his daydream bubble would pop, and he would find himself streaking through the sky to stop some monster from destroying some city.

Just as he was about to do now.

John frowned. Family barbecues were for other people. He was a Green Lantern. With that thought in mind, he took off to meet his teammates in Coast City.

CHAPTER 2

On the planet Aoran, the woman called Maleen gazed at the huge, dark form of the machine in front of her. It looked like a giant seashell made of some strange metal, its gentle but complicated curves leading to a dark, shadowy opening in its center.

"Extraordinary," she said, her voice echoing like a chorus of ghosts in the ancient underground chamber.

"Yes, it is," Jerred agreed. He draped his arm around Maleen's shoulders. "In fact, it is perhaps the most extraordinary device our ancestors ever created."

Jerred wasn't just Maleen's uncle. He was also one of the six elders who sat on the exalted High Council of Escraya.

All six of them were present at that moment. Maleen glanced at the elders, impressed by how calm they looked—even though their stomachs had to be churning with nervousness.

Most of the time, the Council ruled on practical matters—who owed what to whom, and so on. But these days, they were forced to do a great deal more than that. They were forced to take desperate measures in the name of their nation's uncertain future.

That's why they had gathered in this room beneath the capital city of Escrayana, a room that hadn't been opened in hundreds of years. And it was with good reason that it hadn't been opened. The machines made by Maleen's ancestors were too powerful to be tampered with.

It might have been different if any of her people still understood how the devices worked. But not even the wisest of them, the members of the Council, had any knowledge of that.

It was only because of the careful records the Escrayans had kept that they still knew two important things about the machines—what they could do and how to operate them. For the time being, that was all the information they needed.

Abruptly, the seashell-shaped machine came alive.

A ruby red light chased the shadows from the open space in its center.

"Hard to believe," said Maleen, "that this was built more than a thousand years ago."

Jerred stroked his white wisp of a beard. "And it still functions as well as the day it was first activated—a tribute to the expertise of those who came before us."

"Focus it on the coordinates we discussed," said Agrayn, one of Jerred's colleagues on the Council.

Agrayn was a sturdy-looking man with a full head of white hair. Though everyone on the Council was supposed to be equal in authority, he was generally looked to as their leader.

One of the technicians they had brought with them worked the controls in the back of the machine. A moment later, the red light softened and gave way to an image.

But it was fuzzy, difficult to make out. It took a little while for the image to sharpen and become something recognizable.

When it did, Maleen saw the figure of a man. He was flying through the sky like a bird, white clouds streaming past him like a great, frothy river.

"It's him," said Darmac, another of the Council's elders. He was a portly man with a fringe of hair around his otherwise bald skull. "The machine is as accurate as you said it would be, Elder Jerred."

"As accurate as the ancient ones made it," Jerred replied.

Maleen smiled to herself. Her uncle was a modest man who seldom felt the need to take credit for anything.

But it was the figure in the clouds that drew her attention and held it captive. It wore a green and black uniform that Maleen had seen before—with a lantern symbol on its chest, a reference to the amazing source of energy that enabled the figure to fly.

"What is his name?" she asked.

"John Stewart," said Jerred.

"He's one of the Guardians' fiercest warriors," Darmac added.

Maleen knew all about the Guardians and their planet, Oa. After all, her people had been rivals of the Guardians thousands of years ago. They had even gone to war with them and nearly defeated them.

But while the Guardians grew in power and created the Green Lantern Corps, driven by a compulsion to protect and defend planets throughout the galaxy, the Aoranites became complacent. Gradually, so gradually they failed to see it happening, their knowledge of technology withered and their power diminished.

Now they needed someone to protect and defend them from a brutal and merciless enemy called Evil Star. And Maleen's people couldn't ask the Guardians for help because they had declared Aoran off-limits to their Green Lanterns.

She gazed at John Stewart. He seemed so confident, so unafraid. So comfortable with the great power he wielded.

"You see what I mean?" Jerred asked her.

She nodded. "I do."

Earth's Green Lantern was just what they needed.

Maleen's uncle turned to her and spoke softly, so the other elders couldn't hear what he was saying. "Are you certain you want to go through with this, my child?"

She sighed. What choice did she have? The fate of her entire world was at stake.

"I'm certain," said Maleen.

"Good," said Agrayn, who had overheard the conversation despite their whispering. He turned to the technicians who had gathered around the machine's control panel. "You may proceed."

The one who had raised John Stewart's image worked the controls for a moment. Then he looked up and said, "It's done."

Agrayn nodded approvingly. "If I understand the

process correctly, it will take some time before we obtain our champion. In the meantime, we should review what we're to do when he arrives."

Darmac looked at Maleen. "Especially you, my dear."

She nodded. "Don't worry, Councilor. I'll be ready."

CHAPTER 3

John made it to California's Coast City in a matter of minutes. After all, he was used to covering the vast, dark distances between stars. Flying from one city to another was child's play.

He had barely arrived when he caught sight of the high-tech monstrosity that J'onn J'onzz had warned him about. The thing was immense, nine or ten stories tall, and it didn't look anything like an orbiting telescope anymore.

If John were to compare it to something, it would be an ape. After all, it had long armlike limbs in front of it and shorter, more powerful limbs in back. But that was where the resemblance ended.

Solarac—or rather, the thing that *used* to be

Solarac—was made entirely of the supertelescope's component parts. Its body was an accumulation of dark metal plates and cagework. Its arms and legs were long white accumulations of molded plastic. And its head was made up of transformers and coolant containers and computer circuit boards, with huge mirrors where its eyes should have been.

And it was all connected by lengths of thick, black power cable. They ran through every part of the thing, channeling energy to wherever it was needed.

But Solarac wasn't just *using* energy. As J'onn had pointed out, it was *absorbing* energy as well. John homed in on the artificial marauder and saw it grab an electrical line and tear it apart. Then he watched it feed both ends of the line into openings in its upper body.

He could almost imagine the thing sighing as its rampaging hunger was momentarily satisfied. *Nothing like a good meal,* the Green Lantern thought. *But not at the expense of Coast City.*

Those power lines kept hospitals and police stations and a thousand other places alive and operational. Without electricity, people all over the city would be in trouble.

Then John realized that the problem posed by Solarac was even bigger than he had thought—because right before his eyes, the high-tech colossus began to *grow.*

Somehow, it was converting the energy it "ate" into matter—and adding that matter to its already bizarre form. Whatever had caused Solarac to transform itself from an orbital telescope into a towering monster was still at work, still spurring a transformation—and there was no way of knowing where it would end.

That is, if John and his teammates didn't do anything about it. But they would, the Green Lantern vowed. That's why the Justice League had been formed in the first place—to tackle threats too big for any one hero to handle alone.

As he swooped down past the skyline, he saw that at least one member of the League had beaten him to the scene. *The Flash*, John thought with a touch of resentment. The guy in the red suit wasn't called the Fastest Man Alive for nothing.

Looking like little more than a red blur, the Flash was gathering people up and depositing them blocks from the high-tech marauder's path. *Good idea*, the Green Lantern had to admit. The first rule of combat was to make sure all bystanders were out of harm's way.

Descending from the sky, John saw his teammate start to circle the monster's legs as quickly as he could—almost too quick for the eye to see. John understood exactly what the Flash was up to. After all, he had seen him do it before. He was trying to create a whirlwind powerful enough to topple his adversary.

Unfortunately, it didn't seem to bother Solarac. Bending over, the thing swatted at the Flash and only narrowly missed him.

My turn, John thought.

But before he could pound the monstrosity with an energy beam, a winged figure came darting across the space between skyscrapers. It was Hawkgirl, another of his Justice League teammates.

Like J'onn J'onzz, Hawkgirl was a being from another planet. But if one ignored the large gray wings that propelled her through the air, she looked as human as any Earthwoman.

As she reached the lumbering mass of research components, she swung her trademark weapon—a mace that looked as if it would fit perfectly in a medieval museum collection. However, it was actually a highly sophisticated energy weapon created on Hawkgirl's homeworld. It flashed and made a loud *klaannng* as it struck one of Solarac's metal parts.

But it didn't seem to do any damage. In fact, Solarac appeared invigorated by the mace's power—so invigorated that it struck back with blinding speed.

As the winged woman twisted in midair to avoid

the monster's counterattack, John swept in and took her place.

Clenching his jaw, he extended his right hand and willed a blast of the Guardians' green energy at Solarac. It didn't punch a hole in the thing as John had hoped, but at least it got its attention.

Solarac lurched toward the Green Lantern and took a swipe at him, no doubt meaning to snatch him out of the sky. But John swooped away just in time to save himself.

Man, he thought. *This thing is tougher than it looks.*

But so was *he.*

John! someone cried out.

It took him a moment to realize that the voice wasn't in his ear this time. It was in his *brain,* which meant it was a tiny bit faster.

It also meant the voice could have come from only one person—a guy who could communicate without speaking because he was born on a planet where *everyone* did that.

That guy was J'onn J'onzz, the Martian Manhunter. The other Martians had died at the hands of an alien invader, but J'onn had sworn to help the people of Earth avoid the same fate.

The Green Lantern had barely completed the

thought when J'onn came hurtling toward him—with the strikingly beautiful Amazon champion known as Wonder Woman flying right behind him.

At Wonder Woman's birth, she was blessed by the Greek gods with amazing speed, incredible strength, and the power of flight. Raised on an obscure island called Themyscira, she was still learning what life was like in what she called "Man's World."

J'onn and the Amazon banked at the same time and stopped just outside the monster's reach.

I have been in contact with a scientist named Van Domelen, the Martian said with the power of his mind. *He has shed some light on the problem before us.*

"So spill!" the Flash shouted up at him. "Before that thing sucks up every kilowatt in sight!"

J'onn went on, undistracted by his teammate's outburst. *Solarac was exposed to an unusually powerful release of energy in the form of an immense solar flare. It damaged the telescope and also altered its self-repair program, causing Solarac to rebuild itself in a way its creators never intended.*

John saw where the Martian's explanation was going. "And it wants to *continue* rebuilding itself. But to do that, it needs a whopping supply of power."

So it would seem, J'onn replied.

"So," said Wonder Woman, "it's up to us to see that Solarac doesn't *get* that power."

Hawkgirl swooped past John. "So far, we haven't had much success in that department."

"Yeah," said the Flash. "The only one showing signs of slowing down here is *me.*"

We can't beat Solarac one on one, the Martian told them telepathically. *We must work as a team.*

That was fine with John. As the one with the most experience fighting such threats, he took charge of formulating the League's strategy.

"Flash and Wonder Woman," he shouted, "go after its legs. J'onn, Hawkgirl and I will hit it high. With a little luck, we'll send this thing sprawling."

Agreed, came the Martian Manhunter's response.

"All right," the Green Lantern roared, "let 'im have it!"

Everything went the way it was supposed to. Wonder Woman tossed her golden lasso around one of the giant's legs and tugged for all she was worth. Flash did his whirlwind trick again, running circles around Solarac. Hawkgirl hamered away with her mace and J'onn plowed into it with all his Martian strength.

That left John to drive one of his energy beams into the thing's head. Flying as close to the creature as he dared, he released a green barrage that could have leveled a fair-sized building.

But it didn't even slow Solarac down. If anything, it seemed to bolster its energy supply, judging by the speed and power with which it swung its appendage at him.

Again, he was forced to swoop out of the way. And again, the monster missed him. Or did it?

The Green Lantern felt dizzy all of a sudden, disoriented . . . as if he were losing consciousness. It felt as if Solarac had gotten a piece of him after all.

No, he insisted. *It* missed *me.*

Then John spiraled down into a bottomless well, a place as cold as space and twice as dark.

CHAPTER 4

John was falling through darkness. It seemed to him that he had been falling for a long time. Maybe his entire life.

It was quiet as he fell, as quiet as could be. And then, suddenly, he heard voices. They were worried, it seemed to him, though he didn't know why. And they seemed to come to him from very far away.

"Why isn't it working?"

"It *will*. Give it time."

"What if the procedure fails?"

"It's too soon to worry about that."

"But what if it *does*?"

"Then our last hope is gone."

What are they talking about? John wondered.

Then the sound of their argument faded and he began falling again.

As Maleen watched the image of the fallen Green Lantern in the core of the seashell-shaped machine, she frowned at something her uncle had told her.

If the machine worked as it should—as the ancients *meant* it to—John Stewart would remain there on Earth. But at the same time, he would appear on Aoran.

That meant he would be in two places at once. Maleen didn't see how that was possible. For that matter, neither did Jerred. But he had assured her that it would be so.

"All that will be transported here is his essence," her uncle had said. "His ingenuity. His courage. His strength—both the kind in his body and the kind in his ring."

John Stewart wouldn't remember *anything* about his life on Earth. All he would remember was what Agrayn and the others had programmed into the machine—memories of a life on Aoran that the Green Lantern had never led.

If that were all true, the ancients were even more powerful than Maleen had imagined. More than ever, it seemed like a pity that her people had lost the scientific secrets of their ancestors.

"Something's happening!" Darmac cried out.

He was pointing to something in the core of the machine. Maleen followed his gesture and saw that the councilor was right. Something *was* happening.

The image of the Green Lantern was fading. The ruby light was returning to assume its place. And something seemed to be taking shape inside it.

It took Maleen a moment to realize what it was. *A skeleton,* she thought. It was building itself up bone by bone, so quickly that her eyes could barely follow the process.

Then muscles wound their way in and around the bones. Tiny, red pieces of flesh appeared and grew into organs such as kidneys, lungs, and a vibrant, beating heart. A network of tiny nerves spread out from the backbone and formed a wet, gray brain.

A layer of skin spread to cover it all. And that, in turn, was clothed in a green and black uniform. Last of all, a ring appeared.

The process was complete. The being called John Stewart had been reconstituted on the planet Aoran, looking as if he had existed there all his life.

But *was* it John Stewart? Did the body lying there in front of them have his essence in it? His courage and his strength, as her uncle had said? Or was it just a construct of flesh and bone, unable to think or feel for itself?

There was only one way to find out.

"John?" someone said.

He opened his eyes and saw that he was in a room with violet walls, their surfaces sculpted to look like fish scales as they approached the arched ceiling. There was a circle of men around him—men in long, belted garments of various hues, old enough for their hair and beards to have turned white.

He didn't recognize any of them. However, they had an air of authority about them. Authority and wisdom.

"Are you all right, John?" one of the men asked. He had stern-looking features and a full head of hair.

John. That was his name, wasn't it? He remembered that much—if nothing else.

"What happened?" he muttered.

"We don't know," said another of the men, a heavyset fellow with a white fringe of hair around a bald head. "You must have had a run-in with some of Evil Star's henchmen. We found you on the outskirts of the city."

"Thankfully," added a slender man with a white wisp of a beard, "just inside the defense barrier. Otherwise, you might be waking up in Evil Star's prison instead of among friends."

John didn't remember Evil Star or anything else. *Why* didn't he remember?

"You look confused," one of the men observed.

"Of course he does," said the plump one. "He had to have taken quite a beating."

"A beating . . . ?" John repeated numbly.

He shook his head, as if that would help him remember. He didn't *like* feeling so helpless. He didn't like it at all.

Suddenly, a door opened and a woman came through it. John felt his heart skip a beat.

She was beautiful—as beautiful as any woman he had ever seen. But that wasn't what made her feel so special to him. It wasn't the almond shape of her dark eyes or the majestic sweep of her cheekbones. It was something else entirely.

Something he felt he should know, but couldn't quite remember.

"Oh, John," she said. And she threw her arms around him.

He would have liked to embrace her in return, but he didn't know who she was.

"I'm sorry," he said, "do I know you?"

The men standing around them exchanged looks. They didn't seem happy with John's question.

Neither did the woman. She held him away from her and looked at him, her eyes full of surprise and concern. Then she seemed to gather herself.

Turning to the man with the wispy beard, she asked, "What happened?"

The man looked grave as he shook his head. "I'm sorry, Maleen, I don't know. We found him on the edge of the city a little while ago. He was unconscious."

"He must have taken a blow to the head," one of the other men offered. "Such injuries have been known to cause people to lose their memories."

The stern-looking man frowned with concern. "What *do* you remember?" he asked of John.

John thought about it. "Not much. My name." He glanced at the ring on his finger. "That I use this. But I can't remember why or where I got it."

The men looked at each other again.

"Don't worry," said the woman. "We'll help you remember. But for now, let's just go home."

John looked at her. "Together?"

"Naturally," she said. "You *are* my husband."

"I am . . . ?" he said haltingly. He felt a warmth rise in his face. And then, as he realized how fortunate he was to be married to someone so beautiful, he added, "I mean, of course I am."

CHAPTER 5

Agrayn waited until John and Maleen had left the room and were out of earshot. Then he turned to his fellow councilors.

"Apparently," he told them, "our ancestors' machine isn't infallible after all. At least, insofar as the Green Lantern's reprogramming is concerned."

"He doesn't seem to have any of the memories we wanted to give him," Darmac noted.

"Not even the ones that concerned Maleen," said Jerred.

Agrayn frowned as he considered the situation. "It's all right," he said at last. "She'll tell him everything he needs to know."

But that wasn't the worst part of the problem.

"What is it?" asked Jaapho, a tall man with long, white sideburns. "You still seem worried, Agrayn."

"I am," the councilor admitted. "But not about what the Green Lantern doesn't remember. I'm concerned about what he *does* remember."

Jerred saw what he was getting at. "You think if the machine failed to implant new memories . . ."

"Then it may not have been effective in eliminating the *old* ones," Agrayn said, finishing the thought.

"You mean he may remember who he is?" Darmac asked in alarm. "And where he came from?"

"He doesn't seem to," Jaapho noted.

"Not yet," Agrayn agreed. "But in time, who knows?"

"We'll have to watch him," said Jerred. He glanced over his shoulder at the door. "*Maleen* will have to watch him."

Agrayn nodded. "Let us pray that the Green Lantern serves his purpose before his memories return. Otherwise, we may find ourselves with *two* powerful enemies on our hands."

Agrayn was determined to avoid that . . . even if it ultimately meant eliminating John Stewart.

John found himself walking through hallways of pale orange and soft yellow. Like the walls in the room he had woken up in, these were sculpted and met over his head in a series of arches.

They should have looked familiar to him, but they didn't. It was as if he had never seen them before in his life.

He turned to Maleen. "Who's Evil Star? And why was I fighting his henchmen?"

She frowned. "You don't remember Evil Star at all?"

"No," John said. "Tell me about him."

His wife shrugged. "Once, he was a member of a Council of Elders—just like Jerred or Darmac or Agrayn, but in a different city. He was a brilliant scientist, a respected member of the community, with a wife who loved him dearly."

A lot like me, John thought.

"But he became obsessed with death," Maleen continued. "He poured all his wealth and his genius into finding a way to make himself immortal."

Immortal? "Did he succeed?" John asked.

"We don't know. What we *do* know is that he invented a device he calls a starband. It draws light from our sun and other stars and converts it into a terribly destructive form of energy."

"Was he using it against us? Is that what I was fighting against?"

"You're our champion, John. The one who stands between us and the fate that's overtaken the other nations of the world."

"What did Evil Star do to them?" he wondered.

Maleen sighed. "He took them over and proclaimed himself their emperor. All who opposed him were either killed on the spot or thrown into prison. That's how he got the name *Evil* Star."

John scowled. He didn't like the idea of defending one nation when all its neighbors were being crushed to death by a tyrant. It didn't seem right—and he said so.

Maleen looked at him. "That's exactly what you told me this morning. 'It's not enough to keep Escraya safe,' you said. 'We need to free all of Aoran from Evil Star's rule.' "

Just as she said that, John saw that they were approaching a window. His gaze was drawn to it. After all, he didn't know how long he had been unconscious or what time of day it was.

As he got closer to the window, he saw that it was dark out. Then a queasy feeling began to take hold of his stomach. It wasn't just dark. The sky was black.

Completely black.

"Where are the stars?" he asked.

Maleen took his arm. "We haven't seen the stars in more than a year. You don't recall that either?"

John shook his head, feeling more disoriented than ever. "No," he said. "I don't."

"Evil Star's band draws into itself all the energy the stars have to give. There isn't any left to light up our sky."

John felt a muscle twitch in his jaw. He didn't know what bothered him more—that Evil Star had stolen so much from them or that he didn't remember any of it.

"We'll get the stars back," he vowed.

Maleen didn't say anything in return. She just smiled at him. Then she guided him past the window and down the corridor.

The man known to Aoran as Evil Star stood on the balcony of the enormous, sky-shouldering palace his subjects had built for him, and looked down on the city of Ulandir.

The Ulandirans milled in the winding streets far below him, floating globes lighting their way in the otherwise complete darkness. But none of the Ulandirans came too close to his palace. They didn't *dare* for fear of being noticed by him.

It pleased Evil Star that it was so. The people of Ulandir were right to fear and avoid him. After all, he had the power to crush them with a single thought.

He raised his right hand and admired the metal starband on his arm. Once, his colleagues on this city's Council of Elders had laughed at the idea of such a band, just as they had laughed at the idea of his defying death and achieving immortality.

He wasn't immortal. Not yet, anyway. But he had shown the Council how foolish it was to laugh at him.

Once Evil Star had perfected his starband, he had appeared before the Council of Elders and destroyed everyone on it. Then he had crushed anyone else who might have stood against him. And after that, he had pronounced himself Monarch of Ulandira, the nation of which Ulandir was the capital.

But he hadn't stopped there.

Evil Star hadn't invented the starband—or worked continually to improve it—just to become the ruler of a single country. He had greater ambitions than that.

Before long, he had conquered Dashiri, Ulandira's neighbor to the west. Then he seized Chifathia, Ulandira's neighbor to the south. And Asandor. And Wodacron. And most recently, Oldasia.

Nine-tenths of the planet Aoran now bent their

knees to Evil Star. But he wasn't satisfied. Not as long as the nation called Escraya still defied him by remaining free.

Unlike the other populations on Aoran, the Escrayans had taken steps in time to stop him. They had erected powerful energy shields to keep him out of their lands.

It did not surprise him that Escraya would give him the most trouble. Only there did the Council of Elders still study the histories of their ancestors. Only there were the arcane mysteries of the ancients still preserved in some small way.

But for Evil Star to achieve his ambition, Escraya would have to fall. And it *would*, he told himself. The Escrayans would bend to his will like everyone else.

It was just a matter of time.

CHAPTER 6

John Stewart was sitting alone at a table in the house he shared with Maleen, eating breakfast by an open window. It was cool by the window, but not uncomfortably so.

What made him uncomfortable was the *darkness.*

It was daytime. It should have been light out. However, it was barely any different from nighttime. A dark gray, maybe, instead of black, but that was about it.

But then, that made sense. The sun was a star too. If Evil Star was stealing the power of every light in the sky, the sun would be like one big power battery.

John studied the sky and tried to imagine a sun hanging in it. A big yellow ball of light that stung the eyes and made the sky a deep and vibrant blue.

In brightest day . . .

The phrase came to him as if out of nowhere. It seemed so familiar somehow. He was sure he had heard it somewhere. But try as he might, he couldn't remember where.

"John?" said a female voice. It wafted in from the next room.

He recognized the voice as Maleen's. But somehow it still didn't sound as familiar as it should have.

"I'm in here," he said.

A moment later, Maleen appeared. She looked even more beautiful with the coolness of the morning reddening her cheeks.

"I didn't see you when I woke up, so I made myself some breakfast," John said.

"I'm glad you did," she told him. "I had to see to next week's food deliveries. Life goes on, even in a city under siege."

"I suppose," he said.

John didn't like living in fear of an invasion. He didn't like knowing that only a series of transparent energy shields protected Escraya from a brutal tyrant.

"So," he said, taking Maleen's hand to get her attention, "a starband . . . that's Evil Star's weapon, right?"

His wife looked at him. "Yes. It is. But he's created other weapons as well."

"Such as?" John asked.

Maleen sat down opposite him. "Such as his Starlings."

The name didn't ring a bell. But then, nothing else did either. "And what are those?"

"They're artificial life-forms that obey only Evil Star. Separately, they're manageable. But together, they're almost as difficult to defeat as their master."

John nodded. "I see."

"Jerred thinks it was the Starlings who assaulted you and caused your head injury. But of course," said Maleen, "we don't know for certain that's what happened."

John frowned. Obviously, he had his work cut out for him. But somehow he didn't feel afraid. If anything, he was eager for a rematch with Evil Star and his henchmen.

Just one thing puzzled him. "You say Evil Star's starband draws its power from the stars."

"That's right," said his wife.

He held up his ring. "What about *this*? Where does my ring get its power from?" The green circlet on his finger crackled with emerald energy as he spoke.

Maleen smiled a little sadly. "I wish I knew, John. You insisted that your ring's power source be kept a secret, in case any of us were ever captured by Evil Star."

John sighed. Maybe it would come back to him in time. But for now, the source of the ring's power would have to remain a secret even from the man who wore it.

"You still look a little woozy," Maleen observed. "Maybe you should rest."

John shook his head. "No," he said. "I want to go after Evil Star as soon as possible."

His wife looked at him for a moment. Then she nodded. "All right. If that's what you want."

And she showed him how to get to the council chamber.

As soon as Maleen saw the Green Lantern fly off, she opened her personal communicator and contacted her uncle. A moment later, his face appeared on the device's tiny screen.

"Yes, Maleen?"

"John is on his way to the council chamber," she said. She felt a little guilty talking about the Green Lantern behind his back. "He should be there at any moment."

"Thank you for letting us know." Jerred's expression turned thoughtful. "How is he?"

Maleen shrugged. "A little confused, but otherwise well enough."

"Does he suspect what we've done?"

She shook her head. "I don't think so. John seems to accept everything I tell him as the truth."

Jerred nodded. "That's good. But keep an eye on him. His memory may come back to him at any time."

"I'll watch him," Maleen agreed.

"Jerred out." A moment later, his image vanished from the communicator's screen.

She frowned. This assignment she had undertaken for Escraya's sake was more difficult than she had thought it would be. Falsehoods didn't come easily to her.

A breeze blew in through the open window, bringing with it the sweet, fragrant scent of yula blossoms. Maleen smiled. When she was a girl, her family had had a yula grove. She remembered playing in it with her sisters.

That was a more pleasant time—before Evil Star had obtained his unholy power, before he had dimmed the light of the stars. And before she had felt compelled to lie in order to save her world.

The Council's meeting chamber was a large room where pale blue walls twisted higher and higher until they were lost in spiral shapes high above a white flagstone floor.

John's footsteps echoed as he approached the semicircular table where the Council sat. All six members were present, and all six of them seemed eager to hear what he had to say.

"I want to go after Evil Star," he told them. "What kind of resources do I have at my disposal?"

"Resources?" Darmac echoed.

"I'm talking about weapons," John explained. "And people who know how to use them."

Agrayn placed the palms of his hands together. "We *have* no weapons—unless you count your ring."

"And," said Jaapho, "the only soldier we have is *you*."

John frowned. "What about the people?"

Agrayn shrugged. "They fear Evil Star. But then, he has given them ample cause to do so."

"Is it possible they might try to overthrow him on their own?"

Jerred shook his head. "Never. By now, they have all but resigned themselves to his rule."

John nodded. "I see."

"What are you thinking?" Jerred asked.

"I may not be a military strategist, but I know one thing—to overthrow a tyrant, you've got to start at the bottom. And that's where the people are."

Agrayn's eyes narrowed. "Do you have something in mind?"

"We need to do something spectacular," John said. "Something that will give the people hope." He thought for a moment. "What's the most important thing in Evil Star's possession right now? The thing he would hate most to lose or see destroyed?"

It was the Council's turn to ponder. They looked at one another for a while. Then Agrayn spoke up.

"There's the prison in Dashiri."

"Dashiri?" John asked.

Agrayn nodded. "A nation on the other side of Aoran."

"And why is this prison so important?" John asked.

"It houses those who have spoken out against Evil Star and those who tried to spur the people to rise against him."

"He would have killed them all outright," said

Jerred, "but he finds it more useful to keep some of them around."

"As a reminder," Darmac added, "of how futile it is to oppose the likes of Evil Star."

"Then that'll be our target," John decided.

"It's well guarded," Jerred noted.

"We'll need a plan," Jaapho said.

"And a good one," Darmac added.

John felt confident that he could come up with one. "Leave that to *me*."

CHAPTER 7

Maleen stood in a large, open plaza and watched the green and black figure of John Stewart grow smaller and smaller against a dark patch of sky visible between two tall, elegant towers. It wasn't long before she couldn't see him at all.

The technicians who operated the ancients' shield projectors had been alerted that John was coming. They would drop their shields so he could pass, then put them up again to protect Escraya against attack.

Maleen was so intent on watching the Green Lantern's departure, she didn't notice her uncle's approach until he was standing right next to her. He put his arm around her as he had done since she was little.

"May our champion succeed in his mission and come back safely," said Jerred.

Maleen didn't say anything in response to his remark. She was too troubled to speak.

"What is it?" Jerred asked gently.

She looked at him. "I don't like this charade, Uncle. I don't like it at all."

"I don't like it either," he told her. "But it's the only chance we have."

She eyed the starless piece of sky where she had last seen John Stewart. "He's a good man, Uncle. He's a hero. Must we deceive him this way?"

"If we don't," said Jerred, "Evil Star will subjugate us as he has subjugated others. That is unacceptable."

"What if we were to tell him the truth?" Maleen asked. "Maybe he would still decide to help us."

"It's possible," Jerred allowed. "But it's also possible that he would abandon us. After all, he's a Green Lantern, a servant of the Guardians. And if he were to find out how we've tricked him . . ." His voice trailed off, leaving the rest to her imagination.

Maleen sighed. It didn't seem there was any other way to proceed. "I trust you're right."

"I am," said Jerred. "Someday, when this is all over,

you'll see that it was worth it. You'll be satisfied that the end justified the means."

"I hope so," she said.

But until that day came, she would feel bad knowing she hadn't told John Stewart the truth.

As John flew over a chain of dark, brooding mountains, the green glow of his ring the only thing lighting his way, he tried to remember coming this way before.

Maleen and the members of the Council had assured him it wasn't the first time he had flown to Dashiri. But like almost every other memory, it was lost to him.

In any case, John seemed to have made the trip before Evil Star came to power, when the land had looked very different. The lakes and rivers must have shone with reflected sunlight and the forests must have been alive with birds and animals.

If there were any creatures below him now, they were chillingly silent. Clearly, the unrelenting darkness had thrown off their natural rhythms. If it went on much longer, they would probably become extinct, one species after another.

It was another reason John had to take down Evil

Star—as if he needed any reason besides the sadness in Maleen's eyes.

Finally, he swept past the last peaks in the mountain chain. Just beyond them, nestled in a deep valley by a broad river, stood the prison of which the Council had spoken.

It was just as the Elders had described it to him—a dark metal box of a building with a high tower rising from each corner. Actually, each tower was a separate, fully equipped security facility with a powerful force-field projector to keep intruders out and a deadly energy cannon to make sure they didn't call a second time.

No windows. No air vents that John could see. And just one set of doors made of eight-inch-thick titanium, which opened only at Evil Star's command.

Unless the Council had misinformed him, the entire facility was automated—which meant there weren't any guards around. But then, who could Evil Star have trusted with the job? The only underlings he could rely on were his Starlings, and they were too valuable to be stuck here watching prisoners.

The tyrant was better off letting computer-driven machines do that sort of work. And to this point, they had been more than equal to the task. The place had proven itself impossible to get in or out of, impossible to conquer.

John smiled a grim smile. Unless, of course, you were wearing a ring that could *do* the impossible.

Swooping out of the sky, he trained his ring on the nearest of the towers. At first, his beam splattered against the prison's invisible force field. Then he put some more willpower behind it.

The beam struck the field with redoubled force and pierced it. Taking advantage of the opening, John flew through the unseen barrier. And before the energy cannon in the tower could respond to his presence, he drove a shaft of emerald fury in one side of the tower and out the other.

For a moment, a storm of crackling sparks seemed to fill the ruined structure. Then the tower blew itself apart in an immense, deafening explosion and a flash of white light.

One down, thought John. *Three to go.*

Unfortunately, he had been identified as a security threat. As he went after a second tower, the three remaining security stations went after him with sizzling, red energy beams.

John didn't have the luxury of seeing whether the

beams were stronger than his ring's defenses. He had to drop and weave and soar through the air to avoid them.

If there had only been one of the red beams, his task would have been tough enough. But with three of them trying to blast him out of the air, his flying skills were taxed to their limits.

And how long would it be before Evil Star got wind of what was happening and came to investigate? Not long, John imagined. If he was going to accomplish his mission, he had to go on the offensive.

With that in mind, John ascended until he was just below the force field's highest point. The red beams were tracking his flight, not far behind him. But as they converged on his position, he suddenly made a beeline for the base of one of the towers.

Naturally, the beams followed him. In fact, they followed so quickly that the computers directing them didn't register what John was up to—until it was too late.

Just in time, he darted out of harm's way—leaving two of the beams to plow into the base of the third one's tower, shearing it off as neatly as a knife cutting through butter.

The structure toppled, hit the ground, and exploded in a blaze of white. *Two down,* John told himself.

The two remaining towers were diagonally across the prison from each other. As before, they tried to catch him in a cross fire. They were coming close, too, close enough for him to hear the ripping sound the beams made as they cut through the air.

It was difficult to take aim at either tower while he was dodging both energy beams. Therefore, he would have to find a place where he didn't have to do that.

There was only one position that would keep him safe from at least one of the beams—a position that kept him behind one of the towers. Of course, if the prison's security computers had learned from their last mistake, they would stop short of firing at each other—but John would still have only one source of trouble to worry about.

And if the computers *hadn't* learned? That would be just fine with him as well.

As John cut behind one of the towers, he saw the beam from the other tower vanish before it could do damage to its sister structure. It seemed the prison's computers had learned their lesson after all. Unfortunately for them, he had a new one in mind.

With only one shaft of energy to dodge, he was able to aim his ring and fire. Its powerful green beam stabbed through the tower, gutting the machines inside it. A heartbeat later, they went up in a ball of fiery, white light.

That's three, John told himself.

With the third tower destroyed, he no longer had a hiding place. But then, he no longer needed one. With the last surviving tower unleashing bolt after bolt of bloodred fury, John dove and banked and cut from one side of the prison to the other.

All the while, he was jockeying for a closer shot at the tower. And when he got it, he took advantage of it. At this range, his green energy blast didn't just punch a hole in the building. It reduced it to tiny pieces of flying metal.

That left the prison defenseless. John hovered for a moment and scanned the vague line of the horizon. There was still no sign of Evil Star, but that didn't mean he wasn't on his way.

Wasting no time, John trained his beam on a spot in the center of the prison's roof. Its metal was no match for the power of his ring. It gave way as easily as tissue paper would give way to a hot poker, exposing the well-lit insides of the building.

John dropped feetfirst through the hole in the roof, ready for anything. But even before he hit the floor, he saw that the Council's information was correct—there weren't any guards around. Only rows of barred cells extending in every direction. He imagined there were at least a hundred of them in all—and each one contained a prisoner.

Most of them were men, but there were women there as well. At the sight of him, they all pressed their faces to the bars of their cells, their eyes wide with unexpected hope.

"Who are you?" one of them asked.

"How did you get in here?" asked another.

"My name is John Stewart," he told them, "and I come from Escrayana." He used his ring to slice the bars so they could leave their cells. "Unfortunately, there's no time to tell you anything more. Just get out of here and spread the word—Evil Star's tyranny can be overturned. I just proved it."

The prisoners did as he said. As soon as their bars were cut, they streamed out of their cells into the hallways, then down a set of stairs to the ground floor.

But John's work there wasn't finished. After he had satisfied himself that all the prisoners were free, he sailed over their heads and made his way downstairs—where he caught sight of the prison's massive titanium doors.

Somehow, they looked even bigger and thicker from

the inside. The Council had said they were designed to withstand anything people could throw at them.

But whoever had designed the doors hadn't taken John's ring into account. With a mighty blast of green energy, he punched a hole through their titanium surface—a hole wide enough to let the prisoners escape three at a time.

They left the building as quickly as they could, pouring out like water through a broken dam. Most of them headed for the mountains, hoping to lose themselves in them. A few went the other way, toward the city and whatever possibilities it might offer them.

Some of them would likely get caught again. There was nothing John could do about that. But the rest would spread the word about what had happened here in Dashiri.

People all over Aoran would hear the story and realize that Evil Star wasn't all-powerful. They would see that he could be defeated. And if they were brave enough, maybe they would find ways to join in the fight.

At least, that was the idea.

CHAPTER 8

Jerred could have called his niece on her communicator, but he went to visit her in person instead. That way, he believed he would get a more accurate reading of her feelings.

Maleen had always been a sensible individual. That was why the Council had chosen her for this assignment. But judging by the second thoughts Maleen had expressed to her uncle, she had already begun to let emotions come between her and her work.

If Jerred didn't keep an eye on her, she might reveal the truth. And that would jeopardize their world's last chance to save itself from the villainy of Evil Star.

With that in mind, he pressed the illuminated metal plate beside his niece's front doors. A moment later, the doors slid aside for him, revealing the interior of her house.

Jerred had hoped that Maleen would be standing there to greet him. But she wasn't. She was standing by the open window, watching the black and starless sky.

In the corner of the room, a trans-video receiver was silently displaying a message from Evil Star to his subjects. He sent out such messages from time to time, advising the Aoranites of laws he had decided to impose on them.

The tyrant looked as haughty as Jerred had ever seen him. It made his stomach tighten to see such arrogance. No doubt it was having the same effect on every Escrayan—indeed, everyone on the planet.

Except Maleen. She wasn't watching Evil Star's message. She was too intent on the window and the empty sky.

"How are you, Uncle?" she asked without turning.

"The question," he said, "is how are *you*? You look troubled this evening, my child."

The breeze coming through the window lifted her hair. "I am," she said. "I'm worried about John."

"We're *all* worried about him," the councilor told her.

"It's been too long since he left," his niece insisted.

"What if Evil Star got wind of the prison break and moved to stop it?"

Jerred frowned. "We brought the Green Lantern here because he stood a chance of matching Evil Star's power. His ring is an extremely potent weapon."

"But not as potent as Evil Star's starband," Maleen insisted. "And even if John can stand up to the starband, there's the matter of Evil Star's Starlings."

Jerred had to admit that the odds were stacked against their champion. But not wanting to dash his niece's hopes, he made that admission only to himself.

"He'll come back," he said. "You'll see."

His assurance didn't seem to help. Maleen continued to peer at the gloom of the heavens through the window, her delicate features contorted with worry.

Then, all of a sudden, her expression changed. The veil of fear and uncertainty lifted from her face and was replaced with a radiant smile. Maleen raised her hand and pointed.

"Look!" she told her uncle. "Look!"

He moved to her side and followed her gesture. And as he did this, he saw something moving against the darkness of the sky. It was a glow—a *green* glow.

"John," Maleen whispered.

Jerred nodded. "Yes—it's him!"

He couldn't help but be excited as well. After all, the Green Lantern's return to Escrayana was cause for hope.

As the glow got closer, Jerred thought he could see a dark figure in its midst. He had barely become certain of it when, with breathtaking speed, the figure was on top of them.

Before Jerred knew it, Maleen and John Stewart were in each other's arms. They spoke no words. They only stood there and basked in each other's presence.

The councilor saw the look of relief and contentment on his niece's face and couldn't say for sure whether she was acting or not. It certainly appeared that her feelings were genuine. But then, that was the act the Council had requested of her.

"You're back," he observed, shattering the silence.

The Green Lantern turned to him. "I did it. I broke into the prison and freed everyone inside."

Jerred smiled. "That's wonderful. Absolutely wonderful."

And their champion hadn't suffered so much as a scratch. That was wonderful too.

"But I can do more," John Stewart said. "I need to strike again. I just need a target."

"We'll think of one," Jerred assured him.

Their campaign against Evil Star was going every bit as well as they could have hoped. Their champion had succeeded in his first effort and now he was eager to make another one.

Jerred's fears that the Green Lantern would prove reluctant to help them or unequal to the task had turned out to be unfounded. But there was a new concern gnawing at the councilor's stomach—a fear that the Council had asked too much of Maleen and that she would place their plan in jeopardy.

And it chilled him down to his bones.

The man called Evil Star scanned the row of empty prison cells, their doors open wide. Less than an hour earlier, these cells were full of those who had dared oppose his will.

But the prisoners hadn't escaped on their own. Someone had helped them by knocking out the prison's formidable security towers and blasting open the cell doors.

But who possessed that kind of power? Only Evil Star himself. Or so he had believed until now.

"Who *did* this?" he asked himself. His voice echoed hollowly from cell to empty cell.

Evil Star looked back over his caped shoulder at the purple-and-blue-clad Starlings standing at attention behind him. There were a dozen of them, each one nearly a head shorter than their master but a good deal more muscular.

His Starlings stared at him, expressionless, making no attempt to answer his spoken question. But then, he hadn't designed them to come up with answers. He had designed them to crush the opposition without the slightest hint of mercy.

And they would have the chance to do that now.

Evil Star used his mental link with his Starlings to give them their instructions. *Find those who escaped this place,* he told them. *Bring them back.*

He knew that some of the prisoners were skilled at hiding themselves and would be difficult to find. But the tyrant was confident that they would turn up eventually. Rabble-rousers had a way of making themselves known.

Of more concern to him was the identity of those who had enabled the prisoners to escape. But he had a feeling he would run into them as well. And when he did, they would pay for opposing him.

They would pay *dearly.*

John Stewart tapped the oval computer screen with his fingernail. "That's it," he said, referring to the target he had chosen after hours of studying the Council's database.

Maleen, who had gone into the next room to prepare a snack, put her tray down and peered over his shoulder. She didn't speak. She just studied the screen.

"What do you think?" he asked at last.

"This will be more difficult than disabling the prison," Maleen observed in a voice full of concern. "You could be facing more than just automated defense systems."

"You mean Evil Star himself?"

"And maybe his Starlings as well," Maleen said. "Are you ready for that?"

How could John be sure? For all he knew, Evil Star would crush him like a bug. But they were bound to meet at some point. It might as well be sooner rather than later.

"There's only one way to find out," he said.

His wife looked down at him. "Amazing."

"What is?" he asked.

"You," Maleen told him. "It's hard for me to believe that anyone could be so brave."

"You sound as if we've just met," John said.

She smiled. "Silly of me, I know."

He glanced at the tray she had brought in. It held several small, steaming packages of thin, flexible sheet metal.

Because the metal didn't quite come together at the top of each package, John was able to catch glimpses of their contents—prepared foods containing meat and fruit and grains. Like everything else in John's life these days, they didn't look the least bit familiar.

But they *smelled* good. In fact, they smelled *very* good.

"Did you make this yourself?" he asked Maleen.

She nodded. "They're your favorites."

John shook his head. He was about to risk his life a second time against the cruelest and most powerful being he could imagine. And yet he felt like the luckiest man on Aoran.

After all, he had a bright, beautiful wife who adored him as much as he adored her. What else could a man ask for?

"Come on," he said, pulling another chair over so Maleen could sit down alongside him. "I hate to eat alone."

"Of course you do," she said.

Then she sat down beside John and helped him work out the details of his plan.

Chifathia was a sprawling landscape of tall, tapering towers—one of the most impressive cities on all of Aoran. But then, it was the capital of Coranithar, which was the largest and most powerful nation in the southern hemisphere.

Or had been . . . until it fell to Evil Star.

John didn't actually remember that information from the time prior to his head injury. However, he hadn't spent all that time studying the Council's database for nothing.

As he flew closer to Chifathia, which looked like an immense, blue-and-rose-colored island in a dark sea, he noticed the tiny white glows that represented the city's fleet of flying security devices. Before Evil Star conquered Coranithar, the flying machines—also known as "eyes"—had been used by Chifathia's police force to watch for fires and other possible disasters.

Now they were used by Evil Star to keep track of everything that was going on in Chifathia. Instead of helping people and saving lives, the eyes enabled the tyrant to watch for signs of disobedience—which he would, of course, crush the first chance he got.

What John meant to do here could certainly be classified as a sign of disobedience. However, he didn't want Evil Star to get wind of it too quickly. He needed time to carry out his mission.

Fortunately, there weren't any defense towers here as there had been at the prison. But then, why would Evil Star worry about anyone attacking Chifathia . . . or anything in it?

Why indeed, John mused.

He had barely penetrated the city's outer limits when one of the eyes swerved and came flying his way. It looked like a silver hourglass set on its side, both of its flat, circular surfaces equipped with video cameras.

Raising his ring, John speared the device with a stream of green energy no wider than his finger. The eye sparked, sputtered, and fell out of the sky. Almost immediately, a second eye moved toward him to take the first eye's place. He destroyed that one as well.

From that point on, he didn't wait for the eyes to react to him. He went after them one by one, blasting them out of the sky until there weren't any others left to blast.

They might have recorded a distant image of him, maybe a general idea of what he looked like. However, they hadn't seen anything that could tell Evil Star who he was or the nature of his power.

For the time being, that was how John preferred it. The less the tyrant knew about him, the easier it would be for him to carry out another mission—assuming this one turned out to be a success.

Of course, Evil Star would eventually catch a glimpse of him—maybe even in person. But until then, Aoran's champion would remain a mystery to him, an enemy at whom he couldn't strike back.

Weaving his way among Chifathia's towers, John made his way to the heart of the city. According to the Council's database, that was where he would find what he was looking for.

It didn't take him long to locate it. As a matter of fact, it would have been difficult to miss.

The statue was huge, at least a thousand feet high if it was an inch. It was made of something that looked like midnight blue marble with pale purple veins running through it.

Marble was a mineral, John reflected. Evil Star would have to have dragged it out of the earth. To find such an immense block of the stuff, carve it, and transport it here into the midst of a crowded city must have required immense power—not to mention immense skill. Apparently, the tyrant possessed both in great abundance.

Then again, he had the energy of the stars themselves on which to draw. With that kind of force at his disposal, there was precious little that Evil Star couldn't accomplish.

John didn't need that much power to do what he had come here for. And as for skill . . . he hardly needed *any.* It was always easier to destroy than to build.

Descending to a point directly in front of the statue's face, John stopped there and took a moment to study his enemy's countenance. He couldn't see much of it thanks to the mask Evil Star wore, which was carved into the statue as well. It concealed all but his eyes and the lower part of his face.

But what John *could* see was instructive. A proud, jutting chin. Thin lips drawn back in a wolflike grin. An intensity in the eyes that spoke of overwhelming greed and determination.

Eventually, John hoped to wipe that expression from Evil Star's face. But for now, he would have to settle for wiping it from the face of the tyrant's statue.

Raising his arm to shoulder height, John took aim at Evil Star's cruel features and unleashed a blast of green energy. The dark, polished stone split as if he had taken a giant chisel to it, sending fragments spinning end over end to the hard surface below.

But it wasn't the result he had been hoping for. Apparently, the thing was stronger than it looked.

Summoning up more willpower, John drove a wedge of emerald force deep into the center of the statue's forehead. This time, the head cracked in half and both pieces fell away. When they hit the shoulders of the statue, they cracked again and became smaller pieces.

Next, John went after the statue's arms, which were bent at the elbow with their hands planted arrogantly on Evil Star's hips. Severing them at the shoulder and wrist, he watched them plummet and smash to bits on the ground.

By then, the crowds within a couple of blocks of the

square had grown huge. The people of Chifathia had never seen anything like this. They were drawn to the spectacle the way certain insects were drawn to an open flame.

John was glad they were so interested in what he was doing. After all, that was the point of this exercise.

Using his ring's energy like a knife, he sliced through the statue's waist. Then he delivered a blast that slid the statue's torso off its base. As it fell end over end, John's green beam smashed it to powder and bits of debris.

That left only the statue's legs. With a series of emerald energy bursts, John knocked chunks out of them. Finally, he flew up above the barely recognizable structure that was still standing and pounded it into the ground.

By then, a few individuals had separated themselves from the crowd and were addressing their fellow Coranitharans. John swooped lower so he could hear what they were saying. He recognized one of the speakers as a man he had rescued from the prison in Dashiri.

"You see?" the man shouted. "Evil Star isn't all-powerful or he would have prevented the destruction of his statue! He can be defeated!"

John smiled to himself. It was exactly the message he

had meant to get across. It was good to see that word of his efforts was starting to spread around Aoran.

"Together," said the man who had been a prisoner, "we can be more powerful than Evil Star! We can teach him to fear us as we have learned to fear *him*!"

John felt as if he should say something himself. However, it was better to let others do the speaking for him. His legend would grow more quickly if he remained nameless.

As he circled the plaza where the statue had stood, he saw individual Coranitharans lift pieces of debris and send them smashing down into other pieces. They were showing their newfound sense of defiance by following his example.

Satisfied with his work there, John ascended into the empty sky and headed for home.

Jerred stood outside of Agrayn's front door and touched the metal wall pad that would announce his presence there.

He had known Agrayn for a long time. However, he had been invited to Agrayn's home in one of the city's highest towers only once before—to celebrate the birth of the man's granddaughter.

On this occasion, Jerred didn't expect to do any celebrating. Even with the Green Lantern's victory in Dashiri, there was still a great deal for the Council to worry about.

No doubt that was why Agrayn had asked him to visit.

As he thought that, the door opened. "Ah," said Agrayn. "Thank you for being so prompt. Please come in."

Jerred entered the apartment and allowed his host to lead him to a comfortable-looking chair. Agrayn took one on the other side of a low, polished-metal table.

"So," said Jerred, "what did you wish to speak about?"

Agrayn's expression turned somber. "I think you know what I wish to speak about."

Jerred *did* know. "About Maleen."

"She was supposed to be a part of our deception," said Agrayn. "It seems she has become more than that."

"I've noticed it as well," Jerred was forced to admit.

"It's not wise for her to become so involved, my friend."

Jerred shrugged. "You've seen how the Green Lantern acts, how he carries himself—how he springs into battle against terrible odds without a moment's hesitation. Is it any wonder that Maleen has become infatuated with him?"

"John Stewart isn't one of us," Agrayn reminded him sternly. "He's not of this world. He was brought here for one purpose and one purpose only—to rid Aoran of Evil Star."

Jerred sighed. "I know."

"She's your niece," said Agrayn. "Speak to her."

"I have," said Jerred.

"Then speak to her again. For her own sake, see to it that she keeps her emotions in check."

Jerred nodded. "I will do my best."

And he would. He was, after all, a man of his word. But he had seen the look on Maleen's face when the Green Lantern flew through her open window.

If that look was any indication, he would have a hard time making his niece see reason.

Evil Star floated high over the lofty towers of Chifathia, his dark blue cloak snapping viciously under the lash of the wind. He looked down on the ruin that had been his statue. What had once been a mighty tribute to him was nothing more than dust and pebbles.

First the prison, Evil Star thought with a rush of anger, *and now this.* Clearly, he had taken his new-found adversaries too lightly.

When he saw what they had done in Dashiri, he had believed he was still dealing with rebels—a more powerful variety of them, perhaps, but rebels nevertheless. Now he realized that his adversaries were a different breed altogether.

They weren't just trying to free one nation or another from Evil Star's grasp. They were taunting him, trying to expose the chinks in his armor. Trying to make him look bad.

And it wasn't difficult to figure out why.

If they could give the people hope, the people might rise up against him. And they would be much more difficult to crush if they fought him together rather than separately.

Evil Star would still triumph over them in any case. He would still become Aoran's undisputed ruler. But why allow the path of his ambition to become any more arduous than it had to be?

He again eyed the rubble on the ground below and his fists clenched in their purple gloves. He had to destroy the ones responsible for this and he had to do it quickly—so they would never have a chance to mock him this way again.

But Evil Star still had to know who his adversaries were. He still had to find them.

Fortunately, that wouldn't be a problem. In Dashiri, the prison breakout had occurred without witnesses. The only ones who had seen what happened were the prisoners themselves, and they weren't exactly available for questioning.

The situation here in Chifathia was a different one entirely. There had to have been witnesses aplenty. All Evil Star had to do was find them and make them talk.

And he would do that. With pleasure.

At John's insistence, Maleen had agreed to appear before the Council with him.

After all, he had said, her suggestions and her insights had been invaluable to his work. He had come to depend on them every bit as much as he depended on his ring.

So she went with him. But as they entered the chamber, she couldn't help remembering the advice her uncle had given her just before John got back from Chifathia.

"The Council is concerned, my child. And I am more concerned than any of them. You cannot allow yourself to fall in love with the Green Lantern."

She wasn't doing that, Maleen had told him. She

was just doing what she had agreed to do in order to save their world.

But she had lied to her uncle, hadn't she? She *was* falling in love. She hadn't asked for it or expected it, but it was coming over her just the same.

"Welcome," said Agrayn, smiling as he looked at John.

Then he turned his gaze on Maleen. There was just the slightest hint of disapproval in it.

"*Both* of you," he added politely.

"Thank you," the Green Lantern replied, his voice striking echoes off the walls. "I've come to speak with you about our next step."

He looked more confident than ever, Maleen thought. But then, he had a couple of victories under his belt. And the more time he spent on Aoran, the more he studied the Council's database, the better he knew the place.

"We've hit Evil Star and we've hit him hard," John said. "But if we let up now—even a little bit—we'll lose our momentum. We've got to come up with a stunt that will really get the people's attention."

Darmac frowned. "It will be difficult to strike a blow more impressive than those you've already struck."

"Impossible, perhaps," said Jaapho.

"No," said Agrayn, his voice echoing throughout the chamber. "John is right. He must do something that shows once and for all his disdain for Evil Star's power."

"But what?" asked Jerred.

The Council leaned back in their chairs and fell silent. They weren't used to thinking along these lines. For a long time, they had been concerned only with Escraya's defense. Now they were being asked to change direction and go on the offensive.

Maleen considered the question too. In fact, she had been considering it since John returned from Chifathia.

What could John do that would undermine Evil Star even more than the liberation of his prisoners or the loss of his statue? How could the Green Lantern top what he had already accomplished?

Suddenly, an idea came to Maleen. "His communications center," she said in a whisper.

Everyone looked at her. "I beg your pardon?" Agrayn replied.

"His communications center," Maleen repeated. This time, she spoke loudly enough for everyone in the chamber to hear her. "*Evil Star's* communications center."

"What *is* that?" John asked her.

"You've seen Evil Star on the trans-video receiver? When he wants to address all the nations he's conquered?"

John nodded. "Yes . . ."

"He sends out those messages from a communications center in Pejaara, the capital of Poyaaj."

Darmac's eyes lit up. "I see what you mean. John could destroy the facility with his ring. That would leave Evil Star without a way to speak to his subjects."

"But only for a little while," Jaapho said. "He would eventually build another communications center somewhere else. Or perhaps in the very same place."

That wasn't what she had meant. "You don't understand," Maleen told him.

But John did. She could see it in his eyes.

"Maleen's not talking about destroying the place," he said. "She's talking about *using* it."

She smiled. He had come to know her well in the short time they had been together.

"John's right," she told the Council. "I'm saying he can take advantage of the communications center to broadcast a message to the people of Aoran."

"And it will be that much more impressive," said Jerred, picking up her train of thought, "because he will be sending it with the help of Evil Star's own facility."

Maleen nodded. "Exactly."

The Council considered the idea for a moment. "It may be just the thing we need," Agrayn concluded.

"It *is*," the Green Lantern told him. He tossed an approving look in Maleen's direction. "It's perfect."

No, she thought. It wasn't. If it were perfect, there wouldn't be any possibility of John's being destroyed before he could get his message off.

She knew there would be an incredible amount of risk involved in seizing control of the communications center. Of course, John's other missions had involved risk as well. But this one was even more daring, even more defiant.

And having been burned twice, Evil Star would be that much more vigilant. For all Maleen knew, he had set traps for John wherever the tyrant thought John might strike next.

"Then it's settled," said Agrayn. "When do you leave?"

John shrugged. "As soon as I learn what I need to know about the place." He glanced at Maleen. "It shouldn't take more than an hour, I'd think."

"An hour," she confirmed.

Then he would be gone again. And she would be forced to sit by the window and watch for his return— and try to convince herself that he was just an unwitting servant of her people, not a man she was coming to love.

John swept through the seemingly endless darkness, looking for the distant glow that would be the city of Pejaara.

The gloom through which he flew reminded him of the stakes he was playing for. If he failed in his efforts, if Escraya fell like the rest of Aoran, the stars might never be seen again.

It would always be like this. *Always.* Never changing. Children might be born and live their entire lives without ever seeing the sun, without knowing it was ever any different.

In darkest night . . .

The words just popped into John's head—as something similar had popped into his head when he was sitting in his house back in Escrayana. Again, he had the uncomfortable feeling that he had heard it before but couldn't remember any of the details.

Then he was forced to put the subject aside—because as he flew past the shoulder of a mountain, he saw Pejaara. It looked just as the database had described it.

It was an older city, not as elegant as Chifathia or Escrayana. Its towers were smaller and squatter. Still, it had a certain charm to it, a certain hominess, with its soft lighting and its vibrant colors and its winding streets.

The communications center was on the outskirts of Pejaara. A modern building made of metal instead of stone, it looked out of place among its neighbors. But that only made it easier for John to spot.

He wasted no time zeroing in on his objective. Extending his right hand, he sent a blast of green energy plowing through the nearest wall. Then he went plunging through the hole he had made, ignoring the dust and debris that still filled the air.

There were workers inside, open-mouthed and frightened. But John had no time to reassure them, to tell them that he was on their side. Not if he was going to pull this off.

Following the floor plan he had found in the Council's database, he arrowed through one corridor and then another. And finally, he came to the room where the center's broadcasts originated.

There were workers there too—technicians in the midst of checking out their equipment. John wondered if that meant Evil Star was due to arrive soon for another of his trans-video messages.

"Move," he barked.

But the technicians just stood there.

John didn't want to hurt them. He knew they were just acting out of fear of what Evil Star might do to them. But he also didn't have any time to spare.

Training his ring on the technicians, he made a wedge and moved them out of his way. Then, still holding them there, he took up a position at the center's U-shaped, metal control console.

The controls were labeled with symbols, so they weren't difficult for John to understand. One long, red stud turned on the camera in front of him. A blue one activated the communications network and sent the signal out to the rest of Aoran.

First, he swiveled the camera around so it pointed to him. Then he pressed the necessary buttons. When he saw a red light go on above the camera, John knew that his image was being transmitted to cities all over Aoran.

It was time for him to show the Aoranites that the legends were true. There was hope for them. They had a champion in their struggle against Evil Star.

"My name is John," he told them. "I'm a person just like you. And like you, I'm tired of Evil Star's tyranny."

He glanced at the bank of security monitors against

one wall. There wasn't any sign of Evil Star or his Starlings on them. *So far, so good*, John told himself.

"It may have seemed to you that Evil Star is unbeatable. He may have made you believe that you had no choice but to obey him. But I'm not obeying him. I'm *defying* him."

Again, he checked the monitors. Evil Star hadn't shown up yet. He still had some time.

Making use of it, he said, "I'm standing here in Evil Star's own communications center and he hasn't stopped me. Why? Because he can't be everywhere at once."

Finally, John saw something on the monitor. It was just a speck in the sky, or maybe a number of specks all bunched together. But either way, he knew what it meant.

Evil Star was on his way.

"I can't beat him by myself," John said. "But if we all work together, even Evil Star is no match for us. We *can* beat him. We just have to work at it."

And with that, he pressed the button that cut off the broadcast. The specks were gradually growing larger on the screen. Soon they would arrive at the communications center.

John didn't want to meet them inside, where innocent people might get hurt. Dropping the wedge that held the technicians in place, he used his ring to punch a hole in the nearest wall. According to the database, that would get him outside.

When he saw darkness, he knew that the database had been accurate. Darting through the makeshift exit he had created, John rocketed skyward at an angle, trying to put as much distance between himself and the city as possible.

The wind of his passage stung his eyes, but not so badly that he couldn't scan the heavens for Evil Star. According to the monitors in the communications center, the conqueror was somewhere close by.

But where? Where could . . .

No evil shall escape my sight . . .

Now, where had that come from? It was as if the words had been perched on the edge of his mind, waiting for just the right moment to peck at him.

This was getting to be a habit. John knew someone had uttered that phrase to him. But as hard as he tried to remember, he didn't know who or under what circumstances.

Suddenly, he heard something. It was a flapping noise, the sound a flag might make if it were accosted by a stiff wind. *No,* he thought, a chill running up and down his spine—*not a flag.*

A cape.

Looking back over his shoulder, he saw something coming after him, something knifing through the darkness with breathtaking speed. John spun about and braced himself for a headlong assault.

Then the flying figure stopped—just like that, as if braking in midair were the easiest thing in the world—and hovered there. John studied his enemy, ready for anything.

He wore a dark purple uniform, blue boots, and a blue cape that billowed majestically in the wind. And his face was covered with a star-shaped mask the color of blood.

John's eyes narrowed as he said the man's name. "Evil Star."

CHAPTER 11

The conqueror of Aoran smiled a thin, deadly smile.

"That's the name my subjects have invented for me." He tilted his head to one side in a gesture of curiosity. "But who are you?"

John smiled back. "I'm the guy who's going to show you the error of your ways."

Evil Star didn't seem impressed in the least. "Others have tried," he said, "and failed."

"There's always a first time," John said, wishing he was half as confident as he sounded.

Then he leveled a blast of green force at his adversary. But before it could reach the tyrant, a globe of gold-tinted energy formed around him. When the blast struck it, the beam splattered like a stream of water hitting a brick wall.

Inside the globe, Evil Star smiled.

But John wasn't about to accept defeat so easily. Flying closer to his adversary, he battered Evil Star's defenses a second time and a third. Unfortunately, the results were no better. Evil Star remained untouched behind his gold-tinted barrier.

John grunted. Clearly, the straightforward approach wasn't working very well. He had to try a different one.

But before he could think of what it might be, he caught a glimpse of something out of the corner of his eye. Whirling, he saw that it was coming at him out of the sky.

No, he realized. Not *one* something. A number of them.

They were human-looking figures in blue and purple garb, each one smaller than Evil Star by a head but stronger and more muscular-looking. John counted at least half a dozen of them.

And every one of them was headed right for him.

John barely had time to propel himself out of the way before they came streaking past him, buffeting him with the wind of their passage. Before he knew it, they wheeled like a flock of birds and headed for him all over again.

Evil Star laughed. "You thought you had one enemy, but now you see you have many!"

John frowned. These had to be the artificial beings Maleen had told him about. Evil Star's blindly obedient henchmen, who fought for him without question or pause.

His Starlings.

John might have had a chance against Evil Star if it had remained one against one. But with the Starlings thrown into the mix, he would more likely wind up a blotch on the landscape.

He didn't like the idea of running. It went against his nature. But he had to think about more than his pride.

An entire world was depending on him. If Evil Star crushed him and paraded his broken body through the streets, it would destroy everything John had worked for.

He needed to retreat. And he had to do it quickly, while he still had the chance.

"One or many," he told Evil Star, "I'll win in the end!" And with that, he unleashed a blast of emerald energy that dwarfed the ones that had come before it.

Then, while the tyrant was still huddling in his golden globe, John shot off in the direction of Escraya.

In seconds, Evil Star and his Starlings were on John's tail, plowing through the air like blue and purple missiles. Blasts of golden energy erupted in the darkness but never quite caught up to him.

And John kept it that way. He couldn't increase the gap between himself and his pursuers, but he didn't let them narrow it.

Mile after mile, with mountains and lakes and rivers blurring beneath him, he used the power of his ring to propel himself northward. And after what seemed like an eternity, he saw the welcome light of Escrayana crawl over the horizon.

Come on, he urged himself. *Just a little farther.*

Evil Star must have seen the light too, because he redoubled his efforts to bring John down. But as many golden blasts as he sent John's way, not even one reached its target.

John knew he was about to reach Escrayana's outermost shields. If they were strong enough to keep Evil Star out, they would be strong enough to keep *him* out too.

And though the technicians operating the shield projectors would see him coming on their monitors, they couldn't just drop the shields for John. Then they would be letting their enemies in as well as their protector.

Fortunately, John had an advantage. He knew just where the projectors were and how the shields fit together.

With that in mind, he headed for a place Evil Star would have trouble reaching. Maintaining his lead on his enemy, John gave the shield technicians a fraction of a section to drop the individual shield that would let him in.

If they failed to do so, John would be cornered—at his pursuers' mercy. But the technicians *didn't* fail. They dropped the shield for just the amount of time it took to let John in. Then they raised it again in time to absorb a blast of golden star energy.

John turned and hovered for a second, curious to see Evil Star's reaction. The tyrant unleashed a furious barrage at Escrayana's invisible barrier, brightening the sky for a second or two.

But it didn't do anything. The shields held.

Seeing that, Evil Star glowered wordlessly at John. Then, with his Starlings in his wake, he looped around and went back in the direction he had come from.

John watched them go until darkness and distance claimed them. Then he floated down to the house he shared with Maleen, eager to tell her about his latest venture.

Evil Star had flown halfway back to Pejaara before his anger cooled enough for him to consider the matter of his enemy calmly.

Unfortunately, his questioning of the Chifathians hadn't produced much information. All they seemed to know was that the upstart called himself John Stewart—an unusual name indeed.

And while it was rumored that he came from Escraya, it was also said that his home was in Coranithar, or Poyaaj, or Dashiri. It all depended on whom one asked.

Evil Star grunted. He was quite the mysterious fellow, this John Stewart—if that was truly his name.

The conqueror wanted to hate him, but he couldn't. His enemy was doing exactly what Evil Star would have done if their positions were reversed. He was fighting fire with fire.

That ring of his is an interesting item. Probably more of the ancients' magic. When I finally catch him, thought Evil Star, *I'll have to take it apart and see how it works.*

And he *would* catch the fellow. He had no doubt of it.

Evil Star wondered what this John Stewart would

report to the Council in Escrayana. Probably that he had succeeded in his mission—that he had made their great enemy look vulnerable, mortal. And also that they would need to keep the pressure on.

But Evil Star wasn't worried about John Stewart's next move. After all, he meant to apply some pressure of his own.

JL

John was having a dream.

In it, he was fighting someone. But it wasn't Evil Star. It was a pack of men with bulging eyes and strange golden helmets, riding self-propelled one-man fliers and flinging what looked like thunderbolts at him.

There was a city in the distance, a shining city of tall, transparent towers. John knew he had to protect the city and its people, but there was only one of him and there were as many as a dozen of his helmeted adversaries.

He wove his way through them, trying to blast them off their fliers with the beam that shot from his ring. But they were too fast, too good at making twists and turns. And he knew that if he wasn't careful, one of them would nail him with a thunderbolt . . .

Then the flying men were gone as if they had never been there in the first place. John was in a cold place with snowy mountains and a sun so weak and pale that it barely gave any warmth.

There were men and women wearing animal skins, bowing down to John. *Primitive people*, he thought. But he didn't want them to bow down. He wanted them to leave the area because something was coming.

Then he saw something dark and furry crawl over the slope of the nearest mountain. It was a creature with shiny red eyes, a crest on top of its head and gigantic, curved teeth. If it snatched any of the men and women, it would be the end of them.

John couldn't allow that, so he took to the air and sent a beam of green force plowing into the creature. The beam made the creature stagger but didn't knock it down. Then it was the creature's turn to attack.

It took a swipe at him, but he managed to dart out of harm's way. A narrow miss, he thought—too narrow. Then he circled around to take another shot at the creature.

Suddenly, it was gone—just like the men with the bulging eyes and the strange helmets. The snowy mountains and the weak, pale sun and the primitive people were gone too.

John was now standing in a huge chamber in front of a raised platform. The platform supported a council of some kind.

It was made up of little blue men with big heads and wispy white hair, each of them wearing a red and green robe. They looked down on him with serious expressions.

The blue men began speaking to John, telling him something that he felt might be important. But try as he might, he couldn't seem to hear what they were saying. Their voices were echoing too loudly in the chamber, one voice cascading on top of another.

Please, John thought, *one at a time.* But none of the blue men would stop talking. Their voices grew louder and louder, trying desperately to tell him something, until he thought he would go insane.

"No!" he cried out at the top of his lungs.

That's when he opened his eyes and saw that he was in a dark bedroom, his sweat cold on his skin. And he wasn't alone.

"John?" said his wife.

He pulled Maleen close to him. "I thought—"

"What?" she asked.

He shook his head, trying to remember. But the memory was already beginning to fade.

"I was on another planet, fighting men with some kind of thunderbolt weapons. And then I was on a different planet, protecting a primitive tribe from a big, dark beast. And then . . ."

"Then?" asked Maleen.

"Then I was standing in front of a group of little blue men. And they were trying to tell me something."

His wife brushed his cheek with the back of her hand. "You had a nightmare."

He sighed. "Was that it?"

"What else could it have been?" she asked.

John shrugged. "I don't know. It seemed so real. As if I had actually done all those things."

"But how could that be?" Maleen asked. "You've lived here on Aoran all your life. You've never been to another world."

He nodded. She was right, of course. Still, he would have loved to know what the little blue men were trying to say.

CHAPTER 12

Maleen had been awake most of the night.

John had gone back to sleep after his nightmare woke him. But she had been unable to do the same. Unfortunately, he had given her a lot to think about.

The Council had asked her to do a very important job. Part of it was to let them know what John was thinking. That way, they could make sure he didn't turn on them.

Obviously, John's memories were starting to return. That was what his nightmare had been about. His memories were coming back and his mind was trying to decide what to do with them.

It was Maleen's responsibility to tell the Council what had happened. Without a doubt, that was what her uncle Jerred would tell her to do.

But if she did that, they might send John back to Earth. Or if they couldn't do that, they might find some other way to dispose of him. Either way, she would never see him again.

Maleen's uncle had made her promise that she wouldn't let her emotions get in the way of her assignment. But it wasn't just herself she was thinking about. It was her entire world.

John was their only chance to defuse the threat of Evil Star. And she couldn't imagine him turning on them—not even if he *did* remember who he was and realize how they were using him.

Biting her lip, Maleen made a decision. She wouldn't tell the Council about John's nightmare. But was she doing the right thing? Or was she betraying her nation and maybe all of Aoran?

Only time would tell.

JL

John was deep in slumber when he realized that someone was trying to rouse him. He looked up and saw Maleen.

"What is it?" he asked.

"It's Evil Star," she said, her expression tense. "He's back."

"Back?" John echoed.

"He was spotted by city security."

John's heart was pumping as he swept the covers aside and sprang out of bed. "What does he want?"

Maleen shook her head. "I don't know."

John scowled as he crossed the room and opened the closet that held his green and black costume. If Evil Star had wanted to attack Escraya, he would have done it already. So clearly, he wanted something else.

"Be careful," Maleen told him.

John pulled his clothes on. "I'll try," he said.

Then he made his way through their house and flew out an open window. Higher and higher he rose, buoyed by the power of his ring, until he could see past the city's towers and get a view of the vast darkness beyond.

That's when he saw Evil Star.

The tyrant appeared to be alone. If he had brought his Starlings with him, they were somewhere out of sight.

John propelled himself in Evil Star's direction and stopped just short of the city's transparent barrier. Evil Star didn't make a move to defend himself. But then, he knew that Escrayana's shields stood between him and John's ring.

"What are you doing here?" John demanded.

"I came to give you an opportunity."

"Really," said John. "And what kind of opportunity might that be?"

"We don't have to be enemies," Evil Star told him. "You could join me."

John eyed him with suspicion. "You think so?"

Evil Star shrugged. "Why not?"

"Thanks anyway. I don't think I'd be happy as one of your Starlings. I've got a mind of my own."

"You know that's not what I mean," said Evil Star. "I'm not talking about your becoming an unthinking puppet. I'm talking about sitting on my right hand, occupying a position of authority."

"And why would you want me to do that?" John asked.

"Because with the power of your ring, you could help me. And I *know* I could help *you*."

"I don't need your help," John told him.

"*Everyone* needs my help," Evil Star insisted. "I'm going to rule this planet one day. Those who make that day come a little faster will have my gratitude."

"And those who make sure that day *never* comes?"

Evil Star smiled. "You make it seem like you're not tempted. But I know your kind. You possess power.

And those who possess power always want to possess more of it."

"Not always," John said. "I have all the power I need."

Evil Star laughed. "That's what *I* said once. But I was wrong. You can never have enough power."

"You know the problem with you?" John asked. "You've forgotten about the important things in life. You don't remember what it feels like to have the love and respect of other people."

"I'd rather have their fear," Evil Star told him. "It's a great deal more satisfying."

"For you maybe," John said. "But not for me. I wouldn't trade what I've got for anything in the universe."

Evil Star's mouth twisted and he made a sound of disgust. Obviously, his patience had come to an end.

"Then you're a fool," he said. "It's just a pity you won't live long enough to realize it."

And he began blasting away at the invisible shield between them.

At first, John wasn't concerned. He knew how powerful the shield was, how much punishment it could take.

Then Evil Star began to turn it up a notch.

Brilliant, blinding waves of light flowed from his starband, bludgeoning the barrier with the fierce stellar energy accumulated in it, hitting the barrier with so much force that it shivered—and then, amazingly, began to buckle under the onslaught.

John found himself floating backward, uncertain now that the shield would hold against Evil Star after all. His right hand, where he wore his ring, clenched into a fist.

That's when he noticed something new about his enemy's starband. There was a raised strip where before the metal had been smooth. It looked like Evil Star had improved the starband—made it even more powerful than before.

Suddenly, the tyrant desisted. His starband stopped pouring out energy. And he smiled, letting John know that he could have pierced the barrier if he had really wanted to.

Turning his back on John, Evil Star sailed off into the darkness. As Escraya's champion watched him go, his heart sank.

He had planted the seeds of rebellion. He had nurtured them. But now John was afraid they wouldn't have time to grow. He needed to try a new approach or watch Escraya fall to Evil Star—and make the tyrant's victory complete.

Maleen had listened carefully as John sat in their dining area and related his encounter with Evil Star. "Then we're not as safe as we thought we were," she concluded.

John, who was sitting hunched over the table, didn't answer her question directly. As she had come to understand, he didn't like to dwell on the negative side of a situation.

"We need to come up with a way to beat him," he said. "And quickly."

Maleen frowned. It was a lot easier said than done. "He has the energy of the stars at his disposal. How can you beat someone with all that power?"

The Green Lantern sat back in his chair and shook his head. "I don't know. I—"

She looked at him. "John?"

His expression was changing. He was starting to look confident again, excited. "You take his power away."

"Take away the power of the stars?" Maleen asked.

John turned to face her. "I need your help."

"Ask," she said, "and it's yours."

He took her hand and held it in his own. Then he told her what he needed.

There was a small, wooded range of mountains northeast of Escrayana. John sat on its highest peak and searched the inky black sky.

It wasn't long before he saw the glow of Evil Star's starband. Of course, the tyrant could have muted it as he had before and approached under cover of darkness. But this time, he wanted John to know that he was coming.

His Starlings were trailing behind him, partially illuminated by the starband's soft light. John tried to imagine what it was like to serve so blindly, to depend so utterly on the power of another for one's existence.

Let those who worship Evil's might . . .

Once again, he seemed to remember a phrase, but nothing more. And again, he couldn't recall where he had heard it.

John felt that if he thought about it hard enough, the answer would come to him. Maybe someday he would have the chance to do that. But at the moment, he had something a little more urgent on his hands.

Evil Star came to a halt less than ten yards from John, his blue cape billowing about him. His Starlings, on the other hand, moved to surround John the way a pack of wolves might surround a lost sheep. Forming a ring around him, they cut him off from any possibility of escape.

John was all too vulnerable out here in the midst of his enemies, without Escraya's shields to offer him protection. But he couldn't have accomplished anything if he had remained behind the energy barrier.

And if his plan failed . . . and it cost him his life? He resolved not to think about that. He had to concentrate on succeeding, now more than ever.

"So," said Evil Star, "you've reconsidered my offer."

"That's right," John told him.

The tyrant's eyes narrowed in the slits of his mask. "Just like that?"

"I don't blame you for being skeptical," John said. "I was pretty determined not to join you."

Evil Star drifted nearer to him. "What changed your mind?"

John shrugged. "You did."

His enemy studied him. "You mean the wisdom of my words finally sank in?"

That's right, John thought. *Keep coming closer.*

"It wasn't that," he told Evil Star. "I saw what you can do. I can't beat you—and I don't want to die trying."

Closer, John thought. *You're almost where I want you.*

"Before I can trust you," said the conqueror, "you'll have to demonstrate your loyalty to me—by destroying one of the rabble-rousers you set free. Are you prepared to do that?"

"If I have to," John replied.

Evil Star folded his arms across his chest. "Really? You would do that to your allies? I would have expected some reluctance."

He's no fool, John thought. But he was getting close enough for John to see the stubble on the tyrant's unshaven chin—close enough, almost, for John to reach out and touch him.

"Are you sure you're not lying to me?" Evil Star asked. "Laying some sort of trap, perhaps?"

"As a matter of fact," John said, "I *am.*"

Before the tyrant could react, the ground under his feet exploded and a piece of flexible sheet metal erupted to envelop him. It looked like a giant Venus flytrap snapping up an unsuspecting fly.

But a Venus flytrap operated on its own. The piece of metal was driven by the power of John's ring.

Too late, Evil Star raised his right arm, attempting

to vaporize the metal with a blast of stellar power. But by then, John had already used his ring's energy to clamp the sheet around Evil Star, completely encasing him in it.

It hadn't been hard to get the flexible metal. It was the same stuff Maleen had used to hold their food the other day. All John had had to do was find the factory in Escrayana that produced it and obtain a large, uncut sheet.

It seemed absurd that so humble a material would foil the great and powerful Evil Star. And yet, its opacity, strength, and flexibility stood at the core of John's plan.

After all, the tyrant's might came from the stars. And John had just cut him off from his only source of power.

But how long would it take for Evil Star to feel that loss? A second? A minute? An hour?

John had barely asked himself that question when his ring started giving him trouble. All of a sudden it was becoming harder for him to dredge power out of it, harder for him to make it carry out his instructions.

What's going on? he thought.

John didn't remember how he had made the ring, so he didn't know how it worked. But for some reason it was threatening to conk out on him, and at the worst possible time.

If he let up on Evil Star for even a second, the tyrant would burst free of his sheet metal prison. And John couldn't allow that—not when all of Aoran was depending on him.

Evil Star strained hard against the metal, using muscle and energy alike. Holding him in check was like holding back an avalanche. But Escraya's champion didn't give in. He gritted his teeth and forced his ring to keep up the battle.

Evil Star grew hot with pent-up energy as if he were himself a tiny sun. But John's ring drew the heat away from the metal and released it harmlessly into the air.

Come on, he thought, urging on his ring as well as himself. *Just a little longer . . .*

And little by little, to John's great relief, the tyrant's efforts began to diminish. He seemed to weaken, his energy reserves spent in futile attempts to blast himself free.

Finally, he stopped struggling altogether. His power and the heat he had generated were all gone. He was as powerless to move in his metal confinement as any other Aoranite would have been.

It was then that the Starlings began to fall from the sky.

Evil Star's power source had been the stars, but the Starlings' source was Evil Star. Deprived of the energy and guidance with which he supplied them, they couldn't remain aloft. They couldn't even move. All they could do was plummet like huge, blue and purple hailstones.

John watched until the last Starling hit the ground and lay still. Then he pulled away some of the sheet metal covering Evil Star.

Underneath it, the would-be conqueror was pale, drained of all his strength. Barely conscious, in fact. He couldn't even put up a fight as John slipped the starband off his arm.

Without the starband Evil Star was just a man, and an exhausted one at that. With what seemed like the last of his power, John gathered him up in a green bubble and took him back to Escraya as his prisoner.

CHAPTER 13

Word of the Green Lantern's victory had spread across Escraya with the suddenness of a spring rainstorm.

John Stewart had flown above Escrayana with the tyrant in his arms, causing people to point at him and cry out in joy and disbelief. Then he had deposited Evil Star in a building where he could be kept under lock and key, a prisoner of the people he had intended to make *his* prisoners.

But even before the Escrayans saw any of this, they knew that their champion had prevailed—because with Evil Star's starband deactivated, the long-lost stars had winked on again like tiny lights in the sky.

Now there were people all over the place, as if Escrayana was in the midst of a great festival. The streets were choked with revelers. And they were all cheering, all calling out the name of the man who had saved them from a future in chains.

John Stewart, champion of Aoran.

Standing on the balcony that projected from Agrayn's apartment, Jerred nodded with approval. After all, this was what he and the rest of the Council had hoped for. This was the result they had so desperately desired when they called on the secrets of the ancients and summoned Earth's Green Lantern.

Suddenly, the cheers of the crowd grew even louder. A moment later, Jerred saw why. The hero had appeared on a balcony of another tower to acknowledge his people's gratitude.

He waved once, then vanished from sight. After all, John wasn't a glory hound. In his mind, he was just a man who had done his job.

Agrayn, who was standing beside Jerred, watched the cheering crowds as well. But the councilor wasn't celebrating the way the people down below were.

Jerred had an idea why. After all, he was a little worried himself.

"We can't keep him here," Jerred said.

"No," Agrayn agreed. "We can't. He hasn't yet begun

to see the gaps in what we've told him, but he will. And when he does—"

"He'll realize that we've deceived him."

"Exactly. And having realized it, he may turn on us. Besides," said Agrayn, "this isn't John Stewart's world. We borrowed him for a specific purpose. Now it's our responsibility to return him."

Jerred knew that his fellow councilor was right—on both counts. The Green Lantern had obligations elsewhere. He had a *life* elsewhere. It was wrong to make him live the lie they had constructed any longer than was absolutely necessary.

"There is every reason to send him back where he came from," Agrayn added thoughtfully.

Jerred's thoughts turned to Maleen. Despite her promise to him, despite his hopes to the contrary, it was clear that she had fallen in love with John Stewart.

"Every reason but one . . ." he said wistfully.

Maleen gazed at the gaudy sprinkling of stars spread across the dark velvet of the universe. They were so beautiful. She felt privileged just to be able to look at them.

Had they always twinkled that way? she asked herself. Had their light always had that little blue tinge to it?

She couldn't remember. But then, when had she ever really studied the stars? When had she stopped to appreciate them? Like everyone else on her world, Maleen had taken the stars for granted . . . until they were gone.

"Maleen?" said a deep voice, intruding on her thoughts.

A moment later, she felt John's arms around her. Normally, she would have enjoyed the feel of them without reservation.

But her uncle had spoken to her earlier in the day. Agrayn and the Council wanted to return John to Earth.

No, she thought. This *is his home. With* me.

But how could she oppose the Council's wishes? They were the appointed governors of Escraya. Their word was law.

"Yes?" she said, managing a smile.

"My ring's still giving me trouble," John told her. "At least for now. As soon as I figure out how I made it, I'll probably remember how to get it working again."

"Probably," Maleen echoed, though she knew it wouldn't happen.

"You know," said John, "I was thinking . . . Evil Star may not be a threat to us any longer, but we've still got to cope with all the damage he did."

She nodded. "The government buildings . . . and the communications networks. But the nations that own them will take care of them in time."

"I'm sure they will," said John. "But I'm not talking about buildings and networks. What I'm talking about is the way we Aoranites see ourselves. We seem so timid, so happy just to have survived."

"And we shouldn't be that way?" Maleen asked.

"We should try to be *more* than that," he said. He pointed to the lights that had been restored to the sky. "We should reach for the stars. Life isn't about acceptance. It's about *struggle.*"

Maleen turned to look at him. She had felt the same way about her people—even *before* the threat of Evil Star reared its head.

Funny, she thought, *isn't it?* The Aoranites' levels of knowledge and accomplishment had diminished ever since the ancients' defeat at the hands of the Guardians.

And now it was an unsuspecting agent of the Guardians offering them new hope.

"You have a plan?" Maleen asked optimistically.

John shrugged his broad shoulders. "Not a plan,

exactly. Just a few ideas. For instance . . . a space program."

"You mean interplanetary flight?"

"Why not?" he asked.

She frowned. "It's been a long time since the nations of the world got together on anything that ambitious."

"They don't have to get together on it. It can begin right here in Escraya. Then, when the other nations hear about it, they'll want to have space programs of their own."

"But," Maleen said, "Escraya doesn't have any facilities for making spacecraft. And even if we did, we don't have anyone with the expertise to design them."

"Then we'll *make* facilities," John told her, undaunted by her comment. "And we'll develop the expertise."

She sighed. "It won't be easy."

"It's not *supposed* to be," he replied. "It's supposed to be difficult. But that's what makes it worth doing."

Maleen couldn't help smiling a little. Jerred, Agrayn, and Darmac weren't the only wise men on Aoran.

A space program, she thought, reconsidering the notion. *Right here in Escraya.*

Not so long ago, she wouldn't have believed that anyone could accomplish that. But John had beaten the seemingly all-powerful Evil Star. If he could do that, maybe he could start a space program there as well.

Providing, of course, that he had the time. But he didn't, Maleen thought, a lump forming in her throat. John wasn't aware of it, but his stay on Aoran was quickly coming to an end.

Despite her efforts at self-control, she found a tear streaking her cheek. She brushed it away.

"Why are you crying?" John asked, a note of concern in his voice.

"For joy," Maleen told him, lying as skillfully as she could. "I'm crying for joy."

JL

John was walking at a leisurely pace along the sun-warmed streets of Escrayana, on his way to present his ideas to the Council. But his mind was elsewhere.

It was in the starless skies he had seen from his window. It was in the darkness that had seemed destined to go on forever.

Phrases had welled up out of that darkness, coming to him out of nowhere. He had put them aside before, knowing he had to stay focused and alert. But now he could return his attention to them—try to figure out where he had heard them and what they meant. In fact, he had been doing that all morning, albeit without success.

Had he heard them in a poem? In a speech? Or maybe in a song of some kind?

"In brightest day," John muttered out loud.

What came next?

"In darkest night."

So far, so good.

"No evil shall escape my sight."

And the next part?

"Let those who worship evil's might . . ."

For some reason, he couldn't get any further. But there was more. He could feel it in his bones.

Come on, he thought. *You beat Evil Star. You freed Aoran from his tyranny. If you could do* that, *you can do* this.

"Let those who worship evil's might . . . beware my power . . ."

Suddenly, it was as if a mighty dam had broken, unleashing a cascade of images. They flooded John's mind so quickly he thought he would drown in them.

Images of people, of places. And they came with names that sounded strange to him. Superman. Batman. Wonder Woman. The Flash. Hawkgirl. J'onn J'onzz.

The Justice League. John's teeth ground together as he remembered. He was part of the Justice League!

He remembered other people as well, their faces rushing up at him helter-skelter from the swirling depths of his memory. The woman at the fruit stand. The barber around the corner. His old basketball coach.

His friend Isaac. His uncle James.

His father.

His mother . . .

And the Guardians . . . the ones who had given him his ring. The ones who had assigned him a portion of the galaxy and given him the job of protecting it with his life.

They were the little blue men in his dream, weren't they? Now John understood why they had seemed so important to him. When they gave him his ring, they changed his life.

The images assaulted him, bombarded him. Unable to sustain their weight, he stopped and cradled his head in his hands.

"*Beware my power . . .*," he said. Desperate now to dredge it up, he concentrated as hard as he had ever concentrated on anything in his life. "*Beware my power . . .*"

Finally, fighting John all the way, the last bit of it floated to the surface of his mind—and when it did, it gave meaning to all the rest. "*Beware my power . . . Green Lantern's light!*"

No sooner had he said the words than a series of lights exploded in John's brain. He felt himself reeling, his legs unable to bear his weight. The ground rushed up at him faster than he could stop it and smashed him in the side of his head.

But John didn't feel it. In fact, he didn't feel anything.

Even his ring seemed powerless to help him. *What's wrong?* he asked himself, trying to push himself up. *What's happening to me?*

He was still asking when he slid into that deep, dark well again and mercifully blacked out.

CHAPTER 14

Maleen looked at John and wanted to cry.

Her people had found him in the street, moaning about things no Aoranite could have known about. And because of that, the Council had known that memories of his homeworld were coming back to him.

In the end, it didn't matter that she had kept the truth from Agrayn and the others. They had discovered it anyway.

And now John was back in the seashell-shaped machine that had brought him to Aoran. But this time, he had been given a drug that kept him from moving or using his willpower to activate his ring.

The Council was going to send his essence back to

Earth. And when it arrived there, he wouldn't remember any part of his struggle against Evil Star.

True, the ancients' machine had failed to erase John's memories when he arrived on Aoran. But then, it was dealing with a lifetime's worth of experiences. The Council was confident that it would be easier to strip away the few memories he had of their world.

Including his memories of Maleen.

Even in his drugged stupor, John sought her out from the depths of the machine. His expression was the same as when he had awoken from his nightmare.

He looked disturbed. Confused. He didn't know where he was or what had been done to him, or even who had done it.

But John knew *her*, at least. Maleen was certain of it.

He turned to the others in the room—Agrayn and Jerred and Darmac. And he croaked out a word.

"Why?" he asked them.

None of the Council members answered him. They just frowned and looked away.

Maleen wished she could help him, but she couldn't. His fate had already been decided. There was nothing she could do about it.

"I'm sorry," she said, her voice thick with guilt and sadness. "I'm so sorry."

"It's time," said Agrayn, giving the technicians their cue.

As they went to work, the core of the machine began to glow again with a ruby light. John looked around, no doubt aware that something was happening to him against his will.

"Maleen?" he gasped.

Her vision blurred with tears. She tried to say goodbye, but the words caught in her throat.

"Maleen?" John said again.

"It's for the best, John," Jerred told him.

The red glow was getting stronger and more intense by the moment. Maleen wanted to remove John from the machine and throw her arms around him and never let him go.

But she didn't. She held her ground.

When John arrived, the machine had assembled him a part at a time. But the reverse process was different. He didn't disappear layer by layer. He simply began to fade from sight.

Maleen took a deep breath. She had to get the words out before it was too late. Finally, she did it.

"Goodbye," she said, "John Stewart of Earth."

He said her name again. But his voice sounded thin and weak, as if he were calling to her from a great distance.

John was vanishing slowly but surely. Another second and he would be gone altogether.

"I love you," Maleen whispered.

Then the machine was empty. Aoran's champion had departed the same way he had arrived—with not even the slightest idea of what was happening to him.

And Maleen felt as if a piece of her had gone with him.

All was darkness, complete and unbroken.

After a while, a tiny point of light became visible. For a while, it remained that way, small but unyielding, a single glimmer of hope in a sea of despair.

Then it grew bigger. And bigger still. And eventually, it drove away the darkness, revealing a city of high, metal-and-glass towers that rose around him like the points of a shining crown.

Where was he? Even more important . . . *who* was he? Then it all came flooding back to him.

I'm John Stewart, he thought. *I'm a Green Lantern. And I'm here in Coast City to stop the high-tech monster that's sucking up all the power before someone gets hurt.*

Last he remembered he had been hovering high in the air. Now he was lying in the street, propped up on one elbow. But nothing was broken. As always, the

Guardians' ring had done its best to protect its wearer from injury.

Abruptly, his teammates gathered around him.

"Are you all right?" Wonder Woman asked.

John nodded. "Fine."

"You took quite a fall," said J'onn.

"For a second there—" said Flash.

"I told you, I'm *fine*," John insisted.

"Hey," said Flash, holding up his hands in mock defensiveness, "who am I to argue?"

A strange feeling came over John just then—a feeling that he had forgotten something. Something *important*.

But whatever it was, it couldn't have been as important as his duty as a Green Lantern. And right now, his duty called for him to go after the energy-absorbing monstrosity that had laid him out—preferably *before* it stripped the city of its last bit of power.

"Where's that heap of nuts and bolts?" John asked.

Hawkgirl jerked a thumb over her shoulder. "It went that way. Ready to take another shot at it?"

John glanced at her. "I was *born* ready."

Then, his ring blazing with emerald energy, he took to the sky.

But before the Green Lantern had gotten very far, he

knew that something was wrong. Looking at his ring, he could see that its glow was getting erratic—a clear sign that it was running low on energy.

How could that be? He had just recharged it a few minutes earlier while he recited his oath. It should have had enough energy to last him for hours even at its highest level of intensity.

One thing was clear—he wasn't going to do anyone any good by rushing into battle with a useless power ring. Clenching his jaw in frustration, he glided to the ground on the last of his energy reserves.

A moment later, he saw a red and gold blur. Suddenly the Flash was standing in front of him.

"What's up?" asked the Scarlet Speedster.

John shook his head. "I don't know. My ring's out of power all of a sudden."

Usually, the Flash would have answered him with a wisecrack. But not this time. Even he seemed to realize the seriousness of the situation.

"You'd better go after the others," the Green Lantern told him. "Try to knock out that thing without me."

"I guess so," said Flash. "Wish us luck." And he turned to go.

But before he could actually speed off, John changed his mind. "Wait!" he shouted at his teammate.

Freezing before he could take his first step, the Flash looked back over his shoulder at him. "You're going to have to make up your mind, y'know. All this starting and stopping is murder on my boots."

John barely heard him. His mind was running a million miles a minute, even faster than the Flash could sprint.

"I think I've got a way to beat this thing," he said. And he told his teammate what it was, putting the details together as he spoke.

Where had he gotten such an idea? He didn't know. He couldn't remember ever attempting it. And yet, it felt so familiar . . . as if he had just pulled it off the day before.

"I guess it's worth a try," said Flash. Then he sped off in a blur of red and yellow to do his part.

In the meantime, John contacted the rest of the team through the tiny communications links they all wore in their ears. Then he told them his idea. J'onn, Wonder Woman, and Hawkgirl had the same reaction as the Flash—they were willing to try anything at this point.

As the Green Lantern watched from a distance, frustrated at his inability to lend a hand, the Justice League went into action without him. But in a sense, he was with them after all, because it was his plan they were putting into effect.

Flash was grabbing all the metal debris he could carry and piling it in the middle of the street. Moving so quickly he could barely be seen, he had already put together quite a pile.

Wonder Woman's job was to pound the accumulation with trip-hammer force into a rough but unbroken sheet. Because there was so much metal there, it took a while—even for someone as strong as the Amazon.

The Martian Manhunter and Hawkgirl continued to harass Solarac, distracting the monster and keeping it from digging into any more energy sources. They did a good job of it, too. But John knew they couldn't keep it up forever.

And if his plan worked, they wouldn't have to.

Pounding a last pile of debris into shape, Wonder Woman called out to her teammates that she was finished. It was then that Hawkgirl, J'onn, and the Flash came back to join her.

Together, they lifted the enormous piece of metal the Amazon had created, J'onn and Hawkgirl taking the top two corners and Flash and Wonder Woman the bottom two. Then they went after Solarac with it.

The monster didn't have a clue as to what the Justice League was up to. It lumbered along as it had before, focused only on finding more energy sources to feed its immense hunger. By the time it realized there was something blocking the sunlight, it was all but too late.

Whirling, Solarac flung its arm at the huge sheet of metal that J'onn and Hawkgirl were holding between them. But its aim was spoiled by Wonder Woman, who had snared the thing's leg with her lasso and was pulling it off balance as hard as she could.

When the high-tech marauder swiped at Wonder Woman instead, J'onn and Hawkgirl lowered the sheet of metal over its head. Then they crunched it together at the spot where its head met its shoulders to keep it from falling off.

Apparently realizing how it had been fooled, Solarac reached for the metal sheet to tear it off. But before it could do that, the Martian Manhunter rocketed into its midsection. A moment later, Hawkgirl delivered a mighty blow to its leg with her mace—now an ordinary weapon since its owner had deactivated its energy feature. But in Hawkgirl's hands, it still packed quite a wallop.

The monster didn't know who to try to swat first. And before it could figure it out, the Flash ran up and down its body, ripping out wires wherever he could find them.

The Green Lantern didn't think Flash's work would have any real effect on Solarac. After all, the thing was growing new wires almost as quickly as the old ones were torn.

But, like his teammates, the Scarlet Speedster was keeping Solarac busy, forcing it to use the energy it had accumulated. And little by little, the mountain of research components began to slow down, striking with less and less force each time.

Finally, staggered by one last blow from Hawkgirl's mace, the colossus crumpled in a heap of metal and plastic in the middle of the embattled street. The ground trembled under the booming impact. Then all was still.

John's idea had worked, even if his ring hadn't. He could take some pride in that.

Flash was the first one at his side. "Nice going," he told the Green Lantern. "That little brainstorm of yours did the trick."

A moment later, J'onn, Hawkgirl, and Wonder Woman descended beside him.

"How's your ring?" the Amazon asked.

John frowned at it. "I don't know. It's never lost power this way before."

"Hey," said the Flash, "maybe it was Solarac."

They all looked at him.

"You know," he said, "the way it sucked up power from everywhere? Maybe it sucked up the ring's power too."

Hawkgirl smiled. "Actually, that makes sense."

"It does?" asked Flash, looking surprised. Then he caught himself and said, "I mean, of course it does."

It *did* make sense, John thought. His ring was probably just another power source as far as Solarac was concerned.

But for some reason, he had a feeling there was more to it.

EPILOGUE

Maleen watched the image of John Stewart in the core of the seashell-shaped machine.

He was standing alongside a fallen mechanical thing. And he wasn't alone.

There were other heroes on John's homeworld, apparently. One had wings, another blinding speed, and a third had a golden lasso in her hand. Still another had green skin.

As far as Maleen could tell, none of them wielded a ring like John's. But by working together, they had emerged victorious over the mechanical monster.

The Green Lantern himself hadn't lent a hand in his comrades' victory. It seemed his ring had no power left. Maleen wasn't surprised, considering how much energy John had expended on Aoran.

"Maleen?" someone said.

It was Jerred. He left his fellow Council members and joined her in front of the machine.

"We need to leave him now," he said.

She nodded. "I just wanted to make sure he was safe."

Jerred smiled. "You know," he told her, "John was a good man. I'll miss him too."

"No doubt you will," Maleen said. She turned back to the machine and the image of John Stewart in its core. "But not the way *I* will."

ABOUT THE AUTHOR

MICHAEL JAN FRIEDMAN is the author of more than fifty books of fantasy and science fiction, eight of which have appeared on the *New York Times* bestseller list. For years he has been a mainstay of the *Star Trek* book publishing program, contributing critically acclaimed novels that have been widely translated around the world. He also wrote the novelization of the 1997 film *Batman & Robin* (Warner Books) and a series of original novels based on *Lois & Clark: The New Adventures of Superman* (HarperCollins, 1996). In 1995, Friedman co-wrote the *Star Trek: Voyager* television episode "Resistance," which series star Kate Mulgrew cited as her favorite. He has also written more than 160 comic books for DC Comics and Marvel Comics. Friedman lives on Long Island, New York, with his wife and two sons.